DARK WINGS SOARING

Dwain Cassady

ACKNOWLEDGMENTS

I am exceedingly grateful to the folks who helped bring this novel and the whole Dark Wings Trilogy into existence. B. J. Myers-Bradley, Yvette Summerour, and Gary Whatley were willing to read through the manuscript, hunt down typos, and provide feedback that greatly improved the novel. I really appreciate their time and insights. Merilyn Guerry applied her editorial magic in a marvelous way. I remain in awe of her grammatical prowess. I am also grateful to Brandi Doan McCann for the cover design and Becky Franks for the author photo. Their artistic skills are wonderful.

The following websites were instrumental in providing details used for the book:
www.sealaskaheritage.org/programs/language%20resources/tlingit_dictionary_web.pdf
www.google.com/maps/place/Sitka,+AK
www.sitkatrailworks.org

I didn't find pronunciations for the Tlingit names I used for some of the characters. So this is how I pronounced them:
Daséikw: Dah seek.
Shaanáý: Shah a nay
Nadashée: Nad a shé.

Most of all, I want to thank you for reading through the Dark Wings Trilogy and letting me share these stories with you. After you are done, please leave a review on the site from which you purchased the book. Thanks again and enjoy the read!

DARK WINGS

SOARING

CHAPTER 1

"Revenge is devils' work." With that the man turned and walked out of the grocery store.

Sam Hanson creased his brow as he watched the man walk away, long stringy black hair drooping past his shoulders and over the large backpack. Sam observed his scraggly beard when he turned and walked along the sidewalk. He was so thin the backpack threatened to topple him. But he pressed on with a quick stride and was gone.

"That will be seventy-nine eighty-three." The cashier's words pulled Sam back to his mission. "That was Jolly," she said.

"Jolly?"

"That's what we call him. As far as I know, no one knows his name."

"Does he live around here? I've never seen him."

"I have no idea where he lives. He comes in about once a month, buys staples, and hauls them off in that pack."

Sam paid for the groceries and walked outside. He scanned the area but saw no sign of Jolly. "I wonder what he meant." He started to step off the curb, but a Hummer EV3 screeched to a halt right in front of him. A tall, muscular man with close-cropped blond hair got out and slammed the door. He glared at Sam, then walked in.

"How rude can you get," Sam thought as he went to the Tesla. Each time he opened the door to his dad's car, the door to his grief seemed to open as well. Christmas without his dad had been hard. Sam kept telling himself that he needed to move on. His heart seemed to be in no rush.

"Maybe I should trade cars," he thought, but he knew he wouldn't. Driving his dad's vehicle was more meaningful than painful. Light snow started to fall, and it brightened Sam's mood. By the time he got home, he had forgotten about the two irksome strangers at the grocery store.

Sam deposited the groceries on the island at 2:00pm. He heard Evie knocking around upstairs, busy transforming the study into an art studio. Sandra, his mom, was nowhere to be seen. "She's probably napping," he thought as he put away the groceries.

Sam and Evie had elected to live with Sandra for now. It seemed best. They had no income and didn't want Sandra to be alone. Sam couldn't decide if the constant reminders of his dad were helping or hurting. Losing him when his plane was shot down had been bad enough. The presence of his belongings kept the memory fresh.

Quick steps on the stairs announced Evie's approach before she popped into the kitchen in running clothes. "It's snowing!" she announced as she gave Sam a hug. "I'm going running!"

"In the snow?"

"It will be fun!" Evie was out the door before Sam could warn her not to get too cold. He walked outside and watched her disappear down the street. It was past time for the mail to run, so he walked to the mailbox. His heart sank when he saw the letter from the company that had insured Kat's plane.

Setting the rest of the mail on the counter, Sam opened the envelope. It was the settlement check. As he sat in the chair to let his heart settle, an idea began to form. "I could buy another plane and keep Dad's business going." As soon as the thought occurred, he could picture the disapproval on his mother's face. She had already lost her husband in a plane crash. As if she could sense his thoughts, Sandra walked into the kitchen.

"I shouldn't have slept so long, but it was a nice nap. What's that?"

"It's the settlement check for the plane," Sam responded.

"Oh."

Her response told Sam that now was the wrong time to voice his idea. "I'm glad you had a good nap."

"Did you make it by the grocery store?"

"Mission accomplished!"

"Good. Where's Evie? We need to get started on tonight's meal. What time are they coming?"

"Evie is out running. The crew will be here around four since the game starts at five. But you don't have to worry about cooking. We'll handle that."

"I want to help. It will be good to see everyone again. It's been a while."

"Yes, it will. I hope Georgia Tech beats Alabama this year."

Sandra flicked her hand, a signal that, as usual, she didn't want to hear about football.

"Come on, Mom! You have to catch the football bug! At least sit in the den with us while the game is on."

"I will be there, armed with my book, of course. Shouldn't Evie be back by now? I worry about that girl being out by herself."

"It usually takes her twenty-four minutes to run three miles. She's got.. four minutes to go," Sam said after consulting his watch.

"It looks like you worry, too."

"Not as much as I used to. I don't know what I would do without her."

Sam heard his mom's breath catch and saw she was fighting tears. He wondered how long it would take for the raw grief to subside. It had been three months since his dad's death. He wanted the pain to stop. It refused.

Trying to lighten the mood, Sam said, "They had beautiful pecan pies at the grocery store, so I bought two. We won't have to worry about dessert tonight."

Sandra put her arm around Sam's shoulder. "You stay close to Evie. She is too precious to lose."

Sam choked up. "Don't worry. Azul is with her."

Evie popped through the door with cheeks red from the cold air. When Sam and Sandra looked up, Sam could see the recognition on Evie's face.

"I'm going to shower, then we have a party to get ready for! I can't wait to see David and Viviana and James and Tamara!" Evie hustled upstairs.

With Evie back, Sam's heart quickened, and he felt happier. "Evie's right. Do you want to brown ground beef or chop vegetables?"

"I call the ground beef," Sandra said.

Sam's phone rang. "Hey James. How's it going?"

"I'm picking Tamara up at four, so we should be there about four fifteen."

* * *

Tamara glanced at her watch. "I will be able to leave at four. Did you get the appetizers made?" She listened as James explained the items he had prepared for the charcuterie board. "That sounds great! I have clients, so I'll see you at four… I love you, too."

"Sorry about that," Tamara said to the couple who were there to prepare their wills.

"That's fine. You are newlyweds," Joanne Simpson said with a smile. "What does James think about being a house hubby?"

"So far he seems to be enjoying it. It's nice to have one of us free to do all the things there is no time to do when you're working. He plans to work on Jeffery Troutman's boat when fishing season opens up. OK, back to your wills."

* * *

David felt a twinge of guilt as he looked around the office at St. Peter's Episcopal Church. Yet he had to admit that there was more excitement than guilt. When Pastor Watson returned from the vacation she was on at the time of Kat's funeral, she announced that she had been seeking treatment for cancer. Too ill to continue, she resigned at the end of October. The church vestry struggled to find a priest to fill the vacancy. They approached David, and he gladly accepted. He would have to go through the ordination hurdles for the Episcopal Church in the spring.

David's guilt arose because his good fortune came as a result of Pastor Watson's illness. "Somebody has to step in and fill this role," David said to himself. He looked at the bare bookshelves. "I bet I'm the first pastor… priest ever to come to the church with no books," he thought. "It will take me a while to get used to calling myself a priest."

He checked his watch. It was 3:00 pm. He texted Viviana, "I'm going by the hospital and should be there by 4:30. See you soon!"

"Not that you will read it before I get there," he said to the phone.

He remembered very well the struggle over the cell phone. Shortly after the wedding, the owner of the Alaska Raptor Center offered Viviana a job working to rehabilitate injured birds of prey. David bought Viviana a cell phone and insisted that she keep it with her. She did but usually had it turned off. Finally David had convinced Viviana at least to check for messages at the end of the day so she would know if he would be late picking her up.

"If you're not there, I'll just wait," Viviana had said.

"What if the car breaks down and I can't get there for a long time?"

"I will walk."

She always made things so simple. That exasperated David, but down inside he sensed she was right. Why make it so complicated?

He picked up the Bible and the laptop, both gifts from Sandra. They had been Kat's. Looking at the empty office, David thought, "Maybe Viviana is right. We don't need a lot of stuff." He smiled as he unlocked the door to the car, on loan from a parishioner until they could "get on their feet." "I have nothing, but I'm happier than I've ever been."

Viviana applied honey to a hawk's wing and swaddled it as she had Nadashée. Rey stood still beside the bird, cawing gently. "I think you will heal up nicely," she told the hawk and as she put it back into its cage. She delivered a piece of raw chicken as a prize, and the hawk gobbled it down. Rey looked back and forth between the hawk and Viviana.

"OK, mi amigo. You have earned a snack, too." Viviana moved on to a peregrine falcon with a nasty infection from a cut on its breast. Putting the handling gloves back on, Viviana said, "Let's see how you are doing." Before opening the cage, she paused. "I can't believe they actually pay me to do this," she said to Rey. He cawed agreement.

Putting the falcon back into its cage, Viviana noticed David standing across the room. "How long have you been there?"

"Just a few minutes. I enjoy watching you work."

"Is it time to go already?"

"Yes, it's party time!"

Viviana looked at the clock: 4:43. "I'm sorry. I guess I lost track of time again."

"I'm glad you enjoy your job so much!"

Chapter 2

Dusk was starting to settle in when James parked at Tamara's office at 3:55. He was still adjusting to the long nights. Tamara popped out of the office at precisely 4:00. She hopped into the car and gave James a long kiss.

"I missed you," he said.

"I missed you, too."

They arrived at Sandra's and after hugs all around, pitched in with the final steps to get the burrito bar set up. Tamara covered the veggies with foil while James set up the charcuterie board on the coffee table.

At 5:03, David and Viviana arrived.

"Impeccable timing," James teased. "The pregame babble should be ending soon."

The door opened, and Skauty walked in. "You're not starting without me, are you?"

"Hey, Grandpa!" Sam said. Evie beat him to a hug. They settled in the den for the kickoff of the college football championship game.

"The burrito bar is open," Evie announced the moment the first half was over. Sandra closed her book and proceeded to open the crockpot while Evie removed the covers from the vegetables. Sam placed sour cream on the counter, and the burrito building began.

"This is great! We should do this more often," James said as he devoured his first burrito.

"You're right. We should make getting together a regular tradition. I don't want to lose touch now that life is moving on," Evie said.

"Saturday is a big day, Sam. I hope you have been studying your Tlingit heritage. They will grill you, you know." Skauty said.

"I'll be ready," Sam answered. "I've been studying the last few months."

"We'll be there with bells on!" David chirped.

"Do you think there will be any dissension since you're still alive?" Sandra asked.

"Mom!" Sam said.

"Well, it is unusual."

"I don't think so," Skauty said. "It has happened a couple of times before. Besides, if there is contention, now is a good time to sort this out and realize that handing over the reins before one is too old to manage them is a good idea."

"The only problem with that theory is that you're not too old to manage," Evie offered.

"Thanks, but I feel the time is right."

"The ceremony starts at nine, right?" James asked.

* * *

At 9:00 sharp, Skauty addressed the crowd gathered to install Sam as clan leader. "Thank you so much for gathering with us to install Sam Hanson as clan leader for the Sitka clan. I know it is a bit unusual for the current clan leader to be speaking to you from this side of the grave. I am getting old and my energy wanes. I feel it is time to turn leadership over to Sam, who has proved himself worthy in so many ways. Today I am happy to present my grandson, Sam Hanson, for you to consider as the clan leader." Skauty's voice was strong and sure coming over the PA cassytem.

Five clan members and two leaders from other clans formed a panel to ask Sam questions in order to determine his knowledge of Tlingit heritage and ceremonial functions. Syd Skyhawk was head of the panel and spoke first.

"Skauty, it is highly unusual to change clan leaders when the existing leader is still alive, fit, and capable. Why are we doing this now?"

"I have always respected my elders and trusted their wisdom. Now that I am an elder, my wisdom says that someone younger with more energy could better handle our needs. But it's not just my age that leads me to this conclusion.

"The winds brought Sam back to Sitka at a crucial time, and he has saved us from a great tragedy that almost ruined our lives. I believe that the time is right for me to step down as clan leader and that Sam is the one to take up the mantle."

Sam sat listening to the exchange. His palms were sweaty, but he was trying not to let his nervousness show. Skauty's words inspired him. "Maybe this is where I am meant to be," he thought.

"I hadn't thought of it that way," Syd said. "Are there any other statements before we begin the examination?"

"He's a half-breed! I don't think a half-breed should be clan leader!" George Jansen spouted from the right side of the crowd. Four or five people clapped, and George continued. "Having a half-breed as our leader dilutes our Tlingit heritage, and we are already losing ground. I say we keep you as leader. Then we'll find a suitable replacement when you are gone."

"Hear! Hear!" someone said, and a few more people clapped.

Sandi Aspen stood and said, "Skauty has been our leader for a long time, and I trust him. Since he believes this is the right time to change leaders, I wholly support him. And I wholly support Sam. I think he will make an excellent chief."

Skauty resumed, "George, you make the request for Tlingit purity. I say purity is not in the bloodline but in the spirit. Have you noticed Sam's eyes, those amazing blue eyes? The only way he could have those eyes is if somewhere in the past a child was born of a Tlingit and white couple.

"Just about all of us are, most likely, a mixture of one type or another. But that does not diminish us. It makes us stronger. There is greater wisdom in valuing the different than in clinging to the same. Sam has more Tlingit spirit in him than anyone else I know.

That is partly because his spirit was forged in the flames of discrimination like what you are spouting. I submit him as clan leader because I believe he is the right person for this job right now."

Sam's heart swelled. "Could my mixed blood really be an asset? I always thought of it as a curse."

Silence followed Skauty's statement. Sam looked at George, expecting a retort. George was looking off to the side.

After a long moment, Syd said, "Are we ready to proceed with the examination?" No one said anything, and the other panel members nodded their heads.

Sam's throat went dry when the first question came. "What is the duty of the clan leader in regard to clan property?"

"To hold it in trust for the clan," Sam responded.

"Under what circumstances is the clan leader allowed to sell clan property?"

"Never, unless directed to by the council."

"It is our duty to remind any clan leader that holding clan property is a sacred trust carried out on behalf of the entire clan. It does not belong to the leader and is not to be sold, given away, or otherwise disposed of without direction from the council. Next question," Syd said.

Sam sat through the ensuing questions regarding ceremonies and Tlingit traditions. The more he answered, the more confident he became. He didn't realize how much he was sweating until it was over.

Skauty embraced Sam. "You will do a great job."

"Only if you help me," Sam replied. He noticed George Jansen and a few others skulking out the door.

Chapter 3

Skauty's phone rang while Sam and Evie were loading the dishwasher. It was Saturday evening, and David, Viviana, James, and Tamara had come to celebrate Sam's installation as clan leader.

"Hello," Skauty said.

"Hi, this is Stan Aspen."

"Hey, Stan. How are you?"

"Sandi is missing. She stayed late to close up the dive shop. When she didn't come home, I called but couldn't get her. I went back to the shop. Her car is still there, but I can't find her."

"Oh, no! I'm sorry, Stan."

"Hank is the officer on duty, and he recommended I call you. Could we get a search party together?"

"By all means. Of course, Sam is now the chief, but I'll let him know. We'll send a message on the Tlingit app and tell everyone to meet at the shop."

"I was so panicked I forgot. Do I need to call him?"

"No. He's right here with me. I'll tell him."

"Thanks." Skauty disconnected.

"Stan's wife has disappeared. He wants us to get a search party to look for her. I think you had better send word out on the app."

"Of course," Sam said with wide eyes. "How does this sound? 'Sandi Aspen has gone missing. Anyone willing to help with a search party please meet at S and S Dive Shop ASAP.'"

"Perfect," Evie said

"I need a heavier coat if we're going to be outside. We'll go get dressed for the occasion and meet you at the dive shop," David said.

"Same here," James said.

"Why would anyone abduct Sandi?" Tamara asked as she and James headed for the door.

"Robbery?" David suggested as he and Viviana followed them out.

Evie was already racing up the stairs to put on outdoor gear.

Sam joined her. "What good is a search party going to do? It's dark, and we have no idea where to look."

"It's snowing pretty hard, too," Evie said looking out the window. "But we at least have to try. There will be plenty of people to help."

"You're right. It would be hard to live with if we didn't try."

"Do you need a heavier coat, Grandpa?" Sam asked as they came back down.

"No. I'll stay at the shop and help coordinate," Skauty answered.

"OK, let's go," Sam said. "Let's take the Suburban in case we need to haul a crew somewhere." Sam's muscles got tighter and tighter as he drove through the dark snowy night. This was not the way he wanted to start out as clan leader.

Skauty seemed to sense Sam's distress and touched him on the shoulder. "It will be OK, Sam. We will do all we can, and that's all we can do."

"Thanks. I'm glad you're here."

A few cars had already arrived when Sam pulled up. Two police cars were there as well. The shop was a small building, and the parking lot was already filling up, so Sam parked in the lot next door.

They walked up to Hank, who said, "Hey, Chief," and shook Sam's hand. "Thanks for coming out on a night like this."

"Of course," Sam responded. "What can we do to help?"

"We haven't found any clues about what might have happened. Stan said the shop was locked when he got here. It doesn't look like the car has been moved. The security cameras were disabled. Of course, there are no footprints on the asphalt."

Sam looked to Skauty and realized he was waiting for him to respond. "Do you think someone was waiting when she came out of the shop?"

"That would seem logical. Of course, she may just be out for a walk."

"She didn't answer when Stan called, though."

"Wendy is searching the back of the building for footprints. I'll ask everyone to stay clear of that area until she is through. If the snow starts sticking, it will be hard to track prints anyway."

Sam tried to think quickly. "What if we send people out in groups of three along the roads to start with? We need a map and paper to organize which group goes where."

He looked to Skauty for confirmation, and Skauty said, "That's a great idea. I'll use the map to keep track of which roads are assigned."

"Where's Stan?" Sam asked.

"In the shop."

"Did he say if there are any friends close enough that she might have walked to pay a visit?"

"I didn't think to ask that," Hank said.

Sam hurried into the shop and found Stan sitting with his head in his hands. "I'm so sorry, Stan. We'll do everything we can to find her." Stan looked up with fear in his eyes. He didn't say a word.

"Is there a friend nearby that Sandi might have gone to visit?"

"There's Cheryl, but she lives about three miles away. I can't imagine Sandi walking there," he said as he grabbed his phone to call. "Hey, Cheryl. Have you seen Sandi?... I see. I had hoped she might have walked over there... Thanks."

"How about other shops or businesses nearby?"

Stan stared blankly and shook his head. "Have you tried to locate her phone using its GPS signal?"

"Can you do that?" Stan asked and looked at his phone.

"Open it and let me see." Sam located the GPS tracker app on Stan's phone. "What's her number?" He entered it as Stan called it out. The timer turned for a few seconds, and a location popped up. Sam expanded the map until he realized where it was. "It says the phone is here in the shop." They hustled around the shop, looking in and under everything. Stan pulled on the supply room door, but it was locked.

Sam came up as Stan struggled to get the key into the lock. He pulled it open and flicked on the light. Sandi's purse was sitting on a stool in the middle of the room. Stan picked it up and hugged it to his chest.

"What's this?" Sam said, picking up a piece of paper that was under the purse. As he read it, he heard Hank say, "I wish you hadn't touched that."

Sam looked up, not comprehending. His throat went dry. The officer donned gloves and took the purse and paper. "How were these arranged when you found them?"

"The purse was on top of the paper, and they were on that stool," Sam said. Sam watched Hank's eyes widen as he read the note.

"I think we had better get this search started," Hank said.

Sam walked out of the storage room to see Skauty studying a map on the counter. "What is it?" Skauty asked.

"We found her purse and a note. It says, 'Congratulations, Chief. Your nightmare begins."

Chapter 4

"We need to find Sandi in a hurry," Skauty said.

Sam's feet seemed glued to the floor. he couldn't think what to do next.

"Divide people into groups of three, and we'll assign them a route," Skauty directed.

"And don't mention the note," Hank added.

Sam walked outside and saw people everywhere. He was encouraged by the community's response. "Could I have your attention, please," Sam shouted. We're going to send people out in groups of three. Please form a line, and Skauty will assign you a route." Another thought occurred to him. "If you didn't bring a weapon, you should go get it," he told the crowd.

"Evie," Sam called. She appeared out of the crowd with David and Viviana in tow. "Would you three help Grandpa assign the routes?"

"Of course," Evie said. They wrote directions for routes as Skauty called them out and marked them on the map. Sam was busy reminding each group to look around homes and buildings, in sheds, and wherever someone might have hidden Sandi.

It was two and a half hours later when the last group checked back in. No one had found any sign of Sandi or anything else suspicious. Sam felt frustrated and drained. Guilt stung, and the note weighed on his soul as he drove home.

"I feel responsible for this," he said.

"No, Sam. You can't blame yourself," Evie said.

"But the note..." Sam said.

"You have done nothing wrong. I have done nothing wrong. The council approved your election as clan leader. It is the abductor who has done wrong," Skauty said. "Besides, I can't believe any Tlingit would do this to a fellow clan member. I wonder if the note was a decoy to throw us off."

A thought hit hard. "George was quite angry at the meeting today," Sam said. He hit the brakes and whipped the Suburban to the right into a parking lot.

"What are you doing?" Evie nearly yelled.

"I didn't tell Hank about George. The police need to check him out."

When Sam skidded into the S&S parking lot, Hank and Stan were still there. Sam ran over and said, "I forgot to tell you that George Jansen became very angry during my installation ceremony. He said he didn't think a half-breed should be clan leader."

"Thanks, Sam," Hank replied. "We'll have a talk with Mr. Jansen."

Sam waited, but Hank didn't seem to be in a hurry. Sam wanted to storm George's house right then. "Don't you think we should hurry before he has a chance to hide her or do something worse?"

"I appreciate your concern, but I don't think George did this."

"But he was so mad at the installation ceremony. And Sandi spoke up against him."

"Sam, George was here as part of the search party."

Hank's words tempered Sam's zeal to storm George's house. His hope for a quick resolution was crushed. "I see," was all he could manage.

Back in the Suburban, Sam explained that George was part of the search party and that Hank didn't think he could be involved.

"I don't remember seeing George tonight," Evie said.

"I saw him," Skauty said. "I remember sending him out on a route."

Sam's heart sank again. Everyone rode in silence. About halfway home a new thought occurred. "Of course, joining the search party would be a good way to avert suspicion," he said. "I think we should go by his house."

"And I think we should let the police handle this. If George is involved, you could get us and Sandi killed by showing up at his house," Evie protested.

Sam's mind knew there was wisdom in Evie's words, but his heart wanted to charge on. "Can we at least drive by and see if anything looks suspicious?"

"Only if you promise not to knock on the door," Evie said.

Sam slowed to a creep as he approached George's house. He tried not to run off the road while peering into the windows.

"Maybe you should watch the road, and we'll look," Evie said. She had scooted over to the driver's side in the back seat since the house was on the left. It looks like George and a woman are in the kitchen," Evie said.

"I think that's Sarah, his wife. She looks too plump to be Sandi," Skauty observed.

"What are they doing?" Sam asked.

"Getting something to drink, I think," Evie said.

"Does George look nervous?"

"Sam, I can barely see them! I can't read his emotional state!"

"I think we can conclude that Sandi is not here," Skauty said. "I am sure Sarah would never go along with that kind of thing."

Sam turned around down the road and crept along in front of the house again. "What are they doing now?"

"Watching television," Evie said from her perch on the passenger side. "Nothing suspicious here."

"He's still on my suspect list," Sam said.

Back at the house Sam asked, "Do you want to stay over, Grandpa?"

"Thanks, but I would rather sleep in my own bed."

"I don't think I can sleep yet," Sam said as Evie and Sandra went to get ready for bed. Sam sat on the couch and turned on the eleven o'clock news. The lead story was Sandi's abduction.

"A forty-four year-old woman was abducted from her business this evening. Her husband reported that she was closing the S and S

Dive Shop but never came home. Police state they currently have no leads or suspects."

Sam cut off the TV, brooding. "They didn't mention the note. I wonder why." He tried to massage the knots out of his muscles but couldn't quite reach them. His mind was on a continuous loop: "Who could have done this? We have to save Sandi. What can we do next? Who could have done this?..."

Sam shook his head and stretched. "I have to do something to get my mind off of this." Sometime in the night, he fell asleep on the couch and dreamed.

The sound of clinking glass awakened Sam. He found Evie in the kitchen.

"Good morning! I see you slept on the couch."

"I didn't mean to. I had an awful dream."

"Tell me about it."

"I was on top of a mountain. Hundreds of vultures surrounded me. It looked like they were licking their lips. Beaks, I mean. One poked me with its beak and said, 'He's not ready yet.' I ran and ran and started falling down the mountain."

"That's terrible," Evie said. "I think you are stressed out about Sandi's abduction."

"I hope that's all there is to it."

Chapter 5

S am's phone rang while he and Evie were eating bagels and berries for breakfast.

"Good morning, Grandpa."

"Hey, Sam. I think we need to check on Stan this morning."

"I agree. Do you want me to give him a call a little later?"

"No. We need to go in person, let him know we really care."

"OK. What time do you want to go?"

"How about eleven?"

"Sounds great."

"I hope you don't mind missing church. This is important. Oh, and don't bring food. I'm sure Stan will be covered in casseroles before the day is over," Skauty concluded.

Sam disconnected and explained to Evie, "Grandpa wants to pay a visit to Stan this morning."

"That's a good idea. I can't imagine how devastated he is."

"We're going at eleven, so I'll be skipping church."

"I think I'll go. I expect a lot of people will be out today, and I don't want David preaching to a totally empty church."

"I imagine the crowd will be sparse. I could see if Grandpa would be willing to go later."

"No, I think you need to be with Stan. He needs support," Evie said.

Skauty knocked and walked in at 10:45.

"Coffee?" Sam offered, sitting at the kitchen table and nursing the last sips of his cup.

"No, thanks. I had mine earlier. Are you ready to go?"

"I am," Sam said as he rinsed his mug and stuck it into the dishwasher.

"Let's take my car. It's already warm," Skauty said.

As they pulled up to Stan's house, it dawned on Sam how nervous he was. "I don't know what to say," he confided.

"Don't worry. Just being here is the important thing," Skauty said. A police car was parked on the road in front of the house, and Skauty parked behind it.

A haggard looking Stan opened the door.

"Hey, Stan," Skauty said. "How are you holding up?"

"We haven't heard anything. Come in."

"Thanks," Skauty said.

"The police set up a recorder on my phone. They are thinking I might get a call about a ransom."

"We wanted you to know that we are here for you," Sam said, touching Stan on the shoulder.

"Thanks," Stan said, choking up.

Sam heard rustling in the kitchen, then a police officer came out with a cup of coffee. "Hi, Gary Grindle here. There's fresh coffee in the kitchen."

"Sam Hanson," he said. "No word on Sandi?"

Gary shook his head and took a sip. "We're ready if the perpetrator calls."

"I hope we hear something soon. I think I'll sample your coffee making skills."

Gary grinned. "Hold on to your hat for your first sip! It's potent."

Sam walked into the chef-grade kitchen and located the coffee maker. He studied the various options to which the machine could be set. The light was beside Dark Brew. Sam poured a cup and returned to the living area.

"You really expect me just to sit here and wait?" Stan was saying. "I need to be out looking for her."

"Stan, Joe and Jordan are canvassing the neighborhood to see if anyone saw anything that might help. We have asked the owners of businesses in the area to review their security footage to see if they notice anything suspicious. We are casting a much wider net than you could on your own. The one thing that only you can do is answer the phone if the creep calls," Gary explained patiently.

As if on cue the phone rang. Stan froze with a panicked look. Gary jumped to the recorder. "OK, Stan. Go ahead and answer."

"Hello," Stan said.

"Hey, Stan. This is Julie Ford. I'm so sorry about Sandi."

"Thanks."

"I wanted to bring over some food and was just checking to see if you are home."

"I'll be here all day."

"OK, I'll be there in a few minutes."

"Thanks."

Sam could see the frustration on Stan's face. He remembered his own frustration when Skauty was being held by Holmes Harrison.

"I could hardly stand it when Harrison had Grandpa, and we knew where he was. I can't imagine how hard this is."

"Thanks for being here."

Sam sensed rage simmering as Stan paced around the room. Sam couldn't think of anything else to say, so he sat down in the arm chair near the front window and sipped his coffee. He wondered about the note for the thousandth time. "Congratulations, Chief. Your nightmare begins," wormed through his mind and heart relentlessly. The minutes crawled. Sam could hear Skauty talking with Gary.

"We have to do something," Stan said. "I can't stand just sitting here waiting."

"We're doing everything we can," Gary reiterated. "We've had officers out since dawn looking for footprints or any other signs around the shop. We have requested security video from all the shops in the area and are looking for unusual activity. The State Patrol's helicopter is up and searching for signs of someone hiding in the woods. You have a whole team on your side," Gary encouraged.

Sam jumped at a knock on the door. Stan hurried to answer it.

"Hey Stan. I hope this will help," Julie said holding up a casserole dish. Stan started to take it, but Julie pulled it back. "It's still hot. Let me put it on the stove." Without waiting for an answer, Julie bustled in. "It's my famous taco pie. I hope you'll enjoy it."

The aroma woke Sam's stomach and confirmed the presence of a renowned dish. On her way out, Julie touched Stan's arm. "Joe and I will be keeping you in our prayers." With that she left.

The phone rang again, and Stan rushed to answer it. Gary held up his hand for Stan to wait until the recording device was going then gave him a nod.

"Hello."

"Hey, Stan. It's Joe," the voice sounded over the recorder's speaker. "I wanted to let you know that we have finished processing the crime scene. We found no finger prints on the note other than Sam's. There were no signs that they left by foot. So we are concluding that Sandi was taken by vehicle. We are analyzing all the security videos for vehicles that were sighted between the time you left the shop and the time you returned. I have put in a call to the Alaska Bureau of Investigation for assistance. I will keep you apprised as we go along."

"Thanks, Joe," Stan said. Sam wasn't sure what emotion he saw on Stan's face. He seemed in shock, or at least numbed by the strain. Stan stood for a moment then said flatly, "Does anyone want lunch?"

Sam watched as Skauty took the plate he had served, placed it on the table, and pulled Stan by the arm.

"You need to eat," Skauty said.

Stan sat at the table and obeyed.

Having Gary alone in the kitchen, Sam spoke softly, "George Jansen was upset at my becoming the clan leader. He spoke out at the ceremony and Sandi spoke up against him. Grandpa doubts he had anything to do with this, but I'm not so sure. I told Joe last night. Do you know if he has been questioned?"

"Not that I know of. I did hear he helped with the search last night."

"Yeah, but that could just have been a cover to deflect suspicion."

"I'm sure Joe will question him. But I know George. He's hot tempered and flies off at the mouth. I doubt he would do anything this drastic. Besides, why wouldn't he come after you instead of Sandi if he was angry about your being the clan leader?"

Chapter 6

At 3:00 Sunday afternoon, Bryant Stancil arrived by plane from Juneau. He eased his tall lanky frame through Chief Ford's door, pushed a shock of straight brown hair back on his forehead, and extended his hand. "Bryant Stancil, ABI."

"Joe Ford. Thanks for coming so quickly," the chief said as he stood and grasped Bryant's hand. Ford, at five feet eight and stocky, looked up to meet his gaze. "I think we are going to need some help with this investigation."

Without waiting for an invitation, Bryant sat down. "Fill me in."

"Sandi Aspen, a forty-four year-old Tlingit woman, was abducted from her and her husband's dive shop last night. Nothing was taken, and her money and credit cards were still there. We found no prints or other evidence left by the perpetrator. The unusual thing is that the perpetrator left a note." He handed over the note in a clear plastic bag.

Joe watched as Bryant studied it. He saw his brows knit together.

"I think you are right. We are going to need help," Bryant said. "The good news is that the perpetrator seems to think someone he calls 'Chief' is the real target." Bryant stopped and looked at Joe. "Is that you?"

Joe was surprised. "I hadn't thought of that. I assumed it meant our new clan leader, Sam Hanson. He was installed as chief yesterday."

"Hmm," Bryant said, looking back at the note. "Is there anyone else who might be considered a chief?"

"The chief of the fire department... Oh, and the just-retired chief of the Tlingit clan, Skauty Hanson."

"Do you know of any connections between the victim and these people we have identified?"

"Sandi is part of the Tlingit clan. We could find out if any of these potential targets were customers at their shop. I was not a customer. I don't know of any other connections," Joe said, rubbing his hands down his thighs.

"Let's think about you for a minute. Have you made anyone angry lately? Arrested someone who really resented it? Arrested someone for any violent crime?"

"Not that I can think of. We just don't have serious crime around Sitka. There is occasional shoplifting or public drunkenness, but that's about it."

"Can you think of anyone in your personal life who might want to harm you?"

Joe almost immediately answered, "No," but he paused and thought over the people in his life. He didn't want to admit it, but as a police officer he knew he had to. He rubbed his hands down his thighs. "I did have a falling out with my stepson about three weeks ago. He wanted money for something I thought he ought to work and save up for. I wouldn't give him the money. He got angry and stomped out of the room."

"What did he want the money for?" Bryant asked, straightening in his chair.

"He wants to rent an apartment and move in with his girlfriend. He wanted money for the deposit," Joe said, looking at the floor.

"Was he home at the time of the incident?"

"No. He was out with Becky, his girlfriend."

Bryant wrote on his notepad. "We need to corroborate that he was with her. Is there anything else going on in your life that might be of interest in this investigation?"

"I can't imagine Scott doing anything like this. He's not a bad kid. Just a bit lazy," Joe added. "I can't think of anyone else who would be angry with me right now."

"OK. Let's send an officer to talk with the girlfriend. Make sure she is not with your stepson when she is questioned. If Scott was with her at the time of the incident, then we can cross him off the suspect list."

Joe picked up the radio mic and looked over the duty roster. Wendy would be covering Stan's house at this hour, so that left Hank. He got him on the radio.

"Hey, Hank. We need to rule out a potential suspect in the Aspen abduction. See if you can find Becky Troutman. Ask if Scott was with her the night of Sandi's abduction."

"You don't really suspect Scott could be involved in this, do you?" Hank replied.

"Not really, but we need to be sure. He got mad at me the other day. I have Bryant Stancil of the ABI with me, and we're trying to rule out any possibilities. Scott should be at work at the college this afternoon, so you can question her alone. Do you need the address?"

"No, I know where the Troutmans live. I'll get on it right away."

"That should get one suspect off the list," Joe said looking back to Bryant. "Just before you got here, I got a call from Gary, who was stationed at the Aspens' home. He reminded me that George Jansen spoke out against Sam's becoming the clan leader because he isn't full blooded Tlingit. He said that Sandi spoke up against George. George seemed quite angry according to Sam. I was about to send Hank to talk with him when you walked in."

"That's a good idea. Let's send him there after he finishes with Becky Troutman. Has anything else unusual happened in the last few months that might have a bearing on this case?"

"The biggest thing was that Global Food Source came in and tried to force the community to sign on to live in a compound and work the fishing industry. When the village resisted, they even rounded us all up into a pen and were going to ship us off to the wilderness in the interior of Canada."

"What happened?"

"Sam Hanson and some of his friends were able to get us free and send the owner of GFS packing," Joe said with a grin. His grin faded with the realization that GFS might be behind the abduction.

Bryant wrote rapidly on his notepad. "That is definitely a possibility. Was Sandi involved?"

"Not that I'm aware of. She was in the pen with the rest of us."

"Can you think of any other events that might have someone in the community poised to do this? Anything involving the fire chief?"

Joe searched his memory for anything that might have triggered someone to go off the rails and abduct Sandi. He turned and looked out the window as he pondered, knowing that even seemingly insignificant things can set off a landslide. He spun his chair back to face Bryant. "The two big events are the incident with GFS and the installation of a new clan leader. Nothing else comes to mind. I can't imagine why Sandi would be on the radar of anyone from GFS, though."

Bryant finished writing. "That leaves us with two probable targets, the former and current clan leaders. I think we need to put security details on them around the clock until we get this solved." He looked at Joe. "And I would do that starting today."

Joe rubbed his thighs. "We only have two officers on duty during the day and evening shifts and one at night. I have one officer stationed at Stan Aspen's in case the perpetrator calls."

"We're definitely going to need help," Bryant said.

Chapter 7

Sam heard a car pull into the driveway. Out the den window, he saw a Sitka police car. He watched as Joe Ford and a man he did not know got out. Concern flooded Sam's mind. He opened the door before they got there. "Hey, Joe."

"Hey, Sam. This is Bryant Stancil of the ABI. He is here to help with the investigation into Sandi's abduction."

"Nice to meet you," Sam said, shaking hands with both men. "Come in." They sat down in the den.

Evie's footsteps sounded on the stairs. "Who is it?" she said on her way to the den. "Hey, Joe. What are you doing here?" Sandra walked in just behind Evie.

Joe looked to Bryant, who began. "Because of the note, we believe that Sam or Skauty could be the perpetrator's ultimate target."

"What do you mean?" Sam puzzled, struggling to comprehend.

"I expect that Sandi Aspen's abduction is part of a plan to ultimately kill you or your grandfather. And since her abduction happened the day you became chief, I think you are the most likely target."

"Why would they abduct Sandi?" Evie asked.

Joe spoke up. "It is probably a signal that the perpetrator wants to make Sam and the Tlingit community suffer. Since she spoke in support of your becoming chief, that might be why she was targeted."

"We plan to detail officers with you and Skauty Hanson as soon as we can get back up from ABI and the state police," Bryant said

"You mean you're going to have a guard at our houses?" Sam asked.

"Yes. The officer will go with you wherever you go," Bryant explained.

"Do you really think that is necessary?" Sam asked.

"Yes. This perpetrator is serious. He, and I am assuming this person is male, left a note to tell us the plan. It is like he is daring us to try to stop him. We do plan to stop him, but it will take some extraordinary measures," Bryant said.

Sam opened his mouth, but no words came out. He looked at Evie. He tried to process what Bryant had said. "I can't believe anyone in the Tlingit community would do this," he finally said.

"People will do atrocious things in the name of race," Joe said.

Joe's words hit Sam like a punch in the gut. He hadn't thought of his biracial heritage between the encounter with Holmes Harrison and the ruckus at his installation. In fact, he had felt at home in Sitka for the first time he could remember. Sam realized Joe was still talking.

"A lot of people are unhappy with having a biracial clan leader. Not just in our own clan, either. I hear of talk all around."

"What should we do?" Sam managed.

"For now, be wary," Bryant said. "Don't go anywhere isolated. Keep your doors locked and don't open to a stranger. We hope to be able to provide you with a guard by tomorrow."

Sam felt a stab in the center of his soul. "What about Grandpa? I need to bring him here. He lives alone," Sam said, getting up to leave.

"We're heading there next," Joe said to Sam's back as he closed the door.

Joe and Bryant got up. "Remember, keep the doors locked," Bryant told Evie and Sandra as they hustled out to follow Sam.

Sam rushed through Skauty's front door. Skauty looked up from his book. "You seem to be in a hurry."

"You're OK," Sam said with relief flooding his heart.

"Why wouldn't I be OK?"

"The police think Sandi's abduction was just the beginning. They think you or I may be the real target."

"Speaking of police, that looks like Joe pulling in behind you."

"They've come to explain what they think is going on. I want you to come stay at our house till they catch this guy."

Skauty pointed to the shotgun in the corner. "I think I'll be fine."

Joe held up his hand and pretended to knock on the open door.

"Come in," Skauty said.

"Hey, Skauty. This is Bryant Stancil. He's with the ABI."

"Nice to meet you," Skauty said, extending his hand. "Have a seat," he said, gesturing toward the couch.

They sat down, and Bryant went over the implications of the note.

"I appreciate your concern, but I think I'll be fine. I'll keep a deterrent nearby," he said and glanced at the shotgun.

"I don't think we are dealing with someone local," Bryant said. "The total lack of evidence at the crime scene suggests we are dealing with an experienced killer. I suspect someone hired the perpetrator to carry out this mission."

"Skauty, that means this person knows how to deal with someone with a shotgun. I think we need to take extra precautions," Joe added.

"Is there anything I can do to help? We could rally the clan to be on the lookout if we had an idea what we were on the lookout for," Skauty offered.

"The best thing we can do right now is to make it harder for the perpetrator," Joe suggested. "Removing you as a lone, sitting duck is one step. We are hobbled for personnel since it's Sunday. Tomorrow we will begin canvassing grocery stores and outdoor shops for any unusually large purchases and unfamiliar customers."

"I saw two suspicious characters when I was there on Monday. One was a scraggly, skinny guy the grocery store clerk called Jolly," Sam said.

"Jolly is odd, but he has been around a long time. He seems to be a hermit living up the mountain somewhere," Skauty said.

"The other was a rude, entitled soul. He parked his Hummer right in front of the door. I had to walk around it to get to my car. I assumed he was a hunter who felt that he owned the place," Sam continued. He noticed Bryant was taking notes.

"Did you get a good enough look at him to give me a description?" Bryant asked.

"He was tall and muscular with short blond hair. His hair was in a buzz cut. I noticed he had blue eyes when he was staring at me as if daring me to say something about where he parked."

"What color was the Hummer?"

"White."

"I don't suppose you got the license plate?" Bryant asked.

"No, I didn't pay any attention to that."

"Thanks, Sam. That gives us something else to check out. Joe, could you check with car rental places and find out if anyone rented a white Hummer? I'll check with the hunting guides to see if this guy registered with them."

"Of course," Joe said.

"It was an EV3," Sam added.

"Hmm. It will be quiet when it's running," Bryant mused.

Sam looked at Skauty pleadingly. "So, will you come to our house?"

"OK, I don't want you worrying yourself silly about me," Skauty answered. He grudgingly began gathering clothes and toiletries into a bag. "How long am I staying?"

"I have no idea," Sam said. "We can always come back if you need more."

"OK. I'm taking enough for three days. I hope to be back here by then. I don't want to outstay my welcome."

"You're welcome for as long as you want. You know that," Sam said.

Sam's phone rang and a panicked Viviana was on the other end. "Wait, slow down, Viviana. I'm here with the police, so I'm going to put you on speaker. OK, would you mind starting over so everyone can hear?"

"I can't find David! I went to the Raptor Center to take care of the birds. David stayed home to do some chores. When I got back, he was gone."

"Maybe he went for a walk," Sam suggested.

Viviana blurted something in Spanish that Sam knew was not a compliment. Then, "No! There is a note like at the dive shop."

Chapter 8

Sam slid to a stop in front of Viviana and David's house. He and Skauty got out, and Sam ran to the door, which stood open. Sam could see Viviana was frightened. Bryant and Joe followed right behind.

"I'm so sorry, Viviana," Sam said.

"I didn't touch anything," Viviana said. "The note is in here."

The simple three bedroom, two bath house was furnished by the church with donated odds and ends. Viviana led them to the bedroom that was doubling as a study. The note lay on top of the Bible.

Sam reached out to pick it up, but Bryant barked, "Don't touch anything. We will need to dust for prints."

Sam leaned down and read, "The soulless need no spiritual guide."

Joe donned a nylon glove to pick up the note. "I think we're dealing with a sick psycho," he said. "Is this pastor a friend of yours?"

"He's a close friend," Sam said.

Bryant ducked as two birds flew by and landed on the bed, chirping wildly. "Joe, did you leave the door open?"

"I don't think so," Joe said.

"This is Rey and Canto," Sam said. "They are Viviana and David's bird friends. Sam could tell that Bryant was trying to assess his sanity. He started to explain but thought that would just make him look even more crazy.

"Where did Viviana go? I have some questions for her," Bryant said. Viviana walked into the room wearing a deerskin dress and carrying a bow and a quiver of arrows. Sam wished he had a picture of the look on Bryant's face. Then it dawned on Sam what Viviana had in mind, and he cringed.

Bryant asked, "Are you the victim's wife?"

"Yes."

"When was the last time you saw him?"

"About two o'clock this afternoon. Right before I left to go to the Raptor Center."

"Would you mind putting the bow and arrows down?"

Viviana laid them on the bed.

"What were you doing at the Raptor Center?" Bryant continued.

"I fed the birds and dressed some of their wounds."

"So, you work there?"

"Yes."

"Do you know of anyone who would want to harm your husband?"

"Yes."

Sam's eyes widened, and he held his breath. He had no idea someone might have anything against David.

"Who might that be?" Bryant asked.

"It is possible that the owners of MC2 and Global Food Source would want to harm him because of his role in exposing MC2's unlawful disposal of nuclear waste and in spoiling GFS's attempt to take over Sitka."

Bryant looked at Joe. Sam could see he was now trying to assess Viviana's sanity. Joe nodded his head. "What she says is true, at least about GFS. I don't personally know about the MC2 incident.

Bryant's expression intensified. "So, what you are telling me is that we have two possible scenarios going on. This might be a Tlingit vendetta or two of the richest corporations in America may be seeking revenge. That complicates matters," Bryant said and started to pace. "Have any of you seen anybody you recognize from either of those two companies?" All he got was blank stares.

"I haven't," Sam said, suddenly worried even more.

"This sounds like something they would do," Skauty said.

Bryant scratched his head. "But the notes sound like it's a Tlingit matter. I think we still need to keep a lookout for any local people acting suspiciously. We need to check with the airport to see if any planes registered to MC2 or GFS have come in. We're going to need help. Joe, is there anyone who can process this scene for prints?"

"I guess that would be me," Joe said. "I have the equipment in my car."

Viviana picked up her bow and quiver.

"What are you planning to do with those?" Bryant asked.

"I'm going after David," Viviana replied.

"I can't sanction that. The more I learn about this case, the more I fear we are dealing with a skilled assassin."

"That's all the more reason why I need to go now."

"He obviously left by car. He could be anywhere. I don't think you have a chance of finding him," Bryant said.

Viviana held up her arm and called, "Canto."

The wren landed on her forearm, and she looked him in the eye. "I need to find David." The wren flicked his wings and bobbed his head. He flew to the door with Rey right behind. Viviana pulled on a coat and backpack. She turned her cell phone to silent and tucked it into the backpack's pocket.

"Viviana, it's too dangerous, and it's getting dark. At least let me come with you," Sam pleaded.

"You are not ready. You would slow me down," Viviana answered as she walked out of the house.

Bryant stood with his mouth open and looked at Sam. "Did she just talk to that bird?"

"If anyone can find David, it's Viviana," Sam said.

"But I'm sure the perpetrator is armed with more than a bow. And he knows what he is doing. Our best hope is that she doesn't find him," Joe said.

Chapter 9

Viviana walked into the gathering dusk, Canto and Rey flying just ahead. Snow continued to fall and had built up about four inches on the ground. The road and sidewalks were still clear. Canto led them out Indian River Road, right past Sam's house. She noticed his car wasn't back yet. "They are still processing the scene, I guess," she said to Rey and Canto. Canto pressed on past the Hansons' home and took Viviana to the last house at the end of the road.

The house had a large garage off to the side. No lights were on. Viviana looked at Canto for confirmation. Canto flew to the peak of the garage and chirped loudly. Viviana walked past the house and came through the woods to the back. She still saw no lights. She nocked an arrow, skirted along the back yard, and came to the garage.

The side door was locked. She peered inside, but it was too dark to see anything. She turned on the flashlight on her phone and found footprints in the snow leading away from the garage. "Two people. Boots and sneakers," she processed. She looked in the direction indicated by the footprints, then listened. Hearing nothing, Viviana turned and knocked quietly on the garage door. She stepped to the side and held her breath, arrow aimed.

It seemed like she waited forever. No sounds came. "If Canto is right, he must have brought David here and then led him into the woods. That would make sense. I doubt the devil would risk hiding him where a neighbor might hear."

* * *

"We should have stopped her. Surely she will come back when it's dark," Joe worried while he took photos and dusted for prints.

"She won't come back," Sam responded. "She will probably find David. I just hope she doesn't get hurt in the process."

"What makes you so confident she can find him?"

"You don't know Viviana. She lived in a cave on a mountain for many years, and her dad taught her survival skills."

"Oh no," Bryant said and ran fingers through his hair.

Joe announced what they suspected, "No prints. I don't see any evidence that will help us."

"We need to figure out this guy's next move," Bryant said. "Can we connect any dots between the two people who have been abducted?"

"We know Sandi spoke out in favor of Sam's being chief at the meeting. David was recently adopted into the clan. So there's a link in that one supported Sam, who is not full blooded Tlingit, and David, who has no Tlingit blood," Joe said.

Sam cringed when the realization hit. Apparently Bryant noticed and asked, "What is it Sam?"

"Stan and Sandi provided the dive gear that James and Viviana used when they released the fish Harrison had penned up. James also set explosives on Harrison's frigate."

"I see," Bryant said and began pacing again. "If this is a racial matter coming from a Tlingit person, then the next move might be anyone else who is associated with Sam but not of pure Tlingit blood. If this is coming from MC2 or GFS, then the next target might be anyone associated with those events. Who might fit into both categories?"

"Viviana and James fit into both of them," Sam said.

"The Viviana who was just here?"

"Yes."

"She took her cell phone. Call and tell her she may be a target," Joe said, and Sam could hear the concern in his voice.

Sam dialed Viviana's phone, which went directly to voicemail. He started to hang up but decided to leave a message just in case.

When he disconnected, he heard Skauty speaking. "Hey James, it's Skauty. David has been abducted... This afternoon.... Viviana went to find him... Listen, the police have identified you as another potential target. You need to take precautions... I'm staying with Sam for a while. Be careful. Bye."

"I think we have done all we can here. Joe, would you be able to stand guard at Sam's house tonight? I hope we can get some reinforcements tomorrow."

"I was planning on that already."

"Thanks. If you'll drop me by the station, I'll pick up my car and go by the airport. I want to check their logs to see if any planes from MC2 or GFS are registered as having flown in."

"If they are behind this, I doubt the perpetrator would have landed under their name," Joe said.

"I know, but we need to check to be sure," Bryant said as they walked out the door. "Should we lock it? She might come back."

"She left her purse, so she probably doesn't have a key. Let's leave it unlocked," Sam said.

Sam parked in the garage and walked out into the snow. "It seems to be coming down harder. I hope Viviana is OK."

"Me, too," Skauty said.

Sam grabbed the bag and went into the house. "I'm going to send out an update to the clan."

Evie came flying into the den. "What took so long? Are you OK?"

Sam regretted he had not called Evie. "David has been abducted."

"Oh no!" Evie said, putting her hand over her mouth. "We need to get Viviana and bring her here!"

"We can't."

"Why not?"

"She went looking for David."

"You let her go out in this snow? In the dark? Alone?" Evie shouted.

"I couldn't exactly tackle her and hold her down," Sam said, guilt flooding his heart. Evie ran to him, and he embraced her.

"This is getting too scary," she said.

Sam squeezed her tightly.

"They are doing all of this to get to us," Evie said.

The idea that Evie could be a target, too, hit Sam like a freight train. He suddenly felt nauseated. His head started to swim. "I don't think I could take it if they abducted you."

"We will just have to catch this guy before he gets anyone else, then," Evie answered.

Sam's composure ebbed back in. "You're right. Bryant thinks we will have reinforcements tomorrow. Surely they can find this maniac."

A knock on the door startled Sam. He pulled back from Evie and raced to grab the 9mm Luger his dad had kept tucked in the end table. Holding it behind his back, he answered the door.

"Hey, Sam," Joe said, eyeing the arm reaching behind Sam's back. "Mind if I come in?"

"Sure," Sam said.

Evie lit into Joe, "How could four men let Viviana go hunting this monster on her own and in this weather?"

"She didn't give us an option," Joe said.

"Evie, you know Viviana." Sam tried to calm her. "She's more at home in the woods than in a house. She knows what she is doing."

Evie stood with her lips drawn thin. Sam could tell she wasn't buying it. "Still, it's too dangerous. There are some things even Viviana shouldn't try. This is one of them."

"Evie, would you mind helping Joe get settled in? I need to send a message to the clan and let them know what is going on."

"Sure. Joe, what can I get for you?"

Sam sat down and opened his phone. The screen was filled with an alert: Urgent Message! "What in the world? I've never seen that before," he muttered to himself. Sam tried to close it out, but it wouldn't go away. Finally he clicked on it.

An email opened that said, "The bait is being gathered. Three to go. Soon you will need to find me. >>>Solar Wind"

Sam leaned back in his chair and stared at the screen. "I'd better let Joe know about this." He walked to the kitchen where Evie was making coffee, rereading the message as he went.

"Joe, I just got a strange email," Sam said as he handed over the phone.

"That's odd," Joe puzzled. "Who is this from?"

"What is it?" Evie and Sandra asked at the same time.

Joe passed the phone to Evie, and she and Sandra studied it.

Sam took the phone back and tapped on the sender's name, which was, "Solar Wind." "That's even stranger. No email address showed up. This person wants to stay anonymous."

"Here is Bryant's email address. Can you forward that to him?"

Sam tried to tap forward, but it wouldn't open. "Somehow that feature has been disabled. I can send him a screenshot."

After he had copied the text and sent it to Bryant, Sam said, "I'm going to see if I can track this email from my computer." He hurried to the study.

Chapter 10

Before putting up her phone, Viviana checked to be sure it was on silent. She noticed Sam had left a voicemail. "I don't have time for that."

She retraced her steps to the garage and brushed away her prints in the snow as she went. She saw a break in the woods ahead and pushed through the trees. It led to a developed trail. The snow intensified, blanketing the world in white silence. The only sounds were the crunching of the snow under her boots, the flutters of Rey's and Canto's wings, and the babbling of Indian River off in the distance.

Viviana followed the trail east and found the same two footprints joining it from the direction of the house. They were fresh. Viviana quickened her pace, realizing that with this amount of snow falling the prints would soon be filled in. "I wonder how far behind you I am?"

She pushed ahead for a couple of miles. The prints became small indentations. Urgency surged in her blood. She wanted to run but knew not to spend her strength. After about another mile, the prints disappeared. She knelt and looked carefully at the snow but saw nothing. Backing up a few steps, she found another depression. "How did I miss that?"

The depression angled to the left, and Viviana saw prints leading off the trail. She pushed through the tree limbs, blocking them with her bow. Under the trees, the prints had not filled in so much. She followed them northeast. A creek trickled to her left.

She pressed on into the snowy woods. Wariness crept in. "I might be getting close." She tried to look carefully, but the heavy snow and darkness limited her vision. She stopped and listened but heard no footsteps ahead.

After about another mile, the trail began to climb in elevation. It was skirting up the side of a mountain. Rey and Canto kept pace as Viviana followed the trail higher and higher. A cold wind began to blow, and the snow slackened. Within ten minutes, just a few flakes were falling, and she could see stars peeking through the clouds.

"Keep a sharp eye out, mi amigo," she whispered to Rey.

* * *

Sam's hands were shaking as he opened the email from Solar Wind. He began trying to trace the server from which the message was sent. He tried every trick he knew to unmask the source of the email. No luck. He slammed his hand on the desk, and a new email alert pinged.

"I know it's frustrating, but you won't find me by computer. You will have to come in person. >>>Solar Wind"

The email spooked Sam. "This guy knew I was on my computer looking for him."

Sam started when another alert pinged. This one was from Bryant. "Thanks for sending this. I think this further confirms that you are the ultimate target."

Sam looked up as Evie walked in. "Not good news, I see," she said.

"While I was trying to trace this guy, he sent an email saying I wouldn't find him."

"That's creepy. How could he know you were looking for him?"

"I guess there could have been spyware loaded with that email," Sam said. I think this guy knows tricks that I don't." He started to tell Evie about Bryant's email but stopped.

"What else?" Evie asked.

"How can you read my mind like that?"

"I'll never tell," she smiled.

"OK. Bryant said the email makes him more certain that I am the ultimate target." He saw the worry wash over Evie's face. "We're going to be OK. We have Joe here."

"I wish I felt that confident. I don't think I'm going to be able to sleep tonight."

"Yeah, I know what you mean. This is stressful. We just have to trust that Joe and Bryant know what they are doing."

"Speaking of Bryant, there is something about him that is just not right. I don't trust him."

Sam started to dismiss Evie's concern but caught himself. "Why don't you trust him?"

"I don't know. There is something about him that seems fake."

"Well, tonight we have Joe watching over us. We need to at least try to get some sleep so we can face what tomorrow brings."

"I'm afraid tomorrow won't bring good news."

* * *

Viviana continued to follow the prints up in a northeasterly direction. She slowed down a minute to catch her breath. Another two miles went by before she thought she saw a glint of moonlight reflecting off a structure up ahead. She stepped behind a tree and looked out to study the terrain.

The quarter moon and snow gave just enough light to reveal a piece of metal visible through the trees about a quarter of a mile off. She decided to turn east, straight up the mountain, and approach the structure from the high ground. Before setting out, she looked at Rey and Canto and pointed with her bow toward the structure.

Viviana moved as quietly as she could up the mountain. The crunch of snow made it harder. When she was about a hundred yards above her target, she turned east. She wanted to rush to get to David but knew stealth was essential.

She heard a sound coming from the structure. "Was that a door?" She nocked an arrow and continued to maneuver into position above. She could now tell there was a roof covered in snow. She stopped and listened. Hearing nothing, she crept toward the building. Crouching behind a tree, she could see a little shack, really a hut, about ten feet by ten feet. It was nestled against the mountain on its east side. A tree rose from the center.

She resumed moving downhill and stopped when she was even with the roof. She looked and listened. With her next step, Rey let out a loud caw. She ducked behind a tree. Canto's shrill chirp pierced the air over and over.

"I don't get many visitors up here. Welcome to my humble home," a man's voice bellowed from behind the shack.

Viviana remained silent and peered around the tree. She couldn't see him but knew where he was.

"Can I offer you some water?" the man called.

Viviana hustled to the next tree. "No, thank you," she called out.

"Ah, it's Viviana. I have heard about your birds."

Viviana still saw no sign of him. She did not hear him moving, either. "You made the mistake of taking my husband. I want him back." She wanted to keep the man talking.

"You're welcome to come and stay with him right now. Actually, I appreciate your taking the trouble to come up here on your own. You saved me a trip and put me ahead of schedule. I'll be able to leave this cold, forsaken place a day early."

While he talked, Viviana moved to the next tree.

"That's it, come on down and let's talk."

She could hear the threat in his voice.

Rey stopped cawing, and Viviana readied herself.

"Blast you!" the man hollered. Viviana stepped out from the tree. The man had jumped enough when Rey attacked that his shoulder stuck out from the corner of the shack. Viviana released her arrow, and it grazed his shoulder.

She whipped another arrow from the quiver and drew. A rock hit her in the chest, knocking her backward two steps. Before she could recover, the man's big hand locked on the bow and his other fist connected with her jaw. The world went black.

Hector threw the bow down the mountain. Ignoring the wound in his shoulder, he aimed his revolver at Viviana's heart. "No, that would be too easy. I want you to suffer."

Chapter 11

At 8:45 on Monday morning, Sam opened his phone. The urgent message icon was back. The email said, "Four are taken. One to go. It's almost time. >>>Solar Wind"

Sam dropped the phone. "Oh, no!"

Joe and Evie converged on the kitchen. "What is it?"

"I think he got Viviana," he said, holding out the phone.

"That says four are taken. Viviana would just make three," Joe observed. "Who could be number four?"

"James! We have to get over there!" Evie said and ran for her purse and coat. "Don't just stand there! Come on!"

"Um, don't you think we could just call and see if James answers?" Sam asked.

Evie stopped and glared at Sam. He understood that somehow she knew. "You're right. Let's go."

"I think it would be wise to call first," Joe said.

"Trust me," Sam said. "Evie can just see things like this. She is right. You can call, but you won't get an answer."

Skauty came down the stairs as Sam was putting on his coat. "Where are you off to so early?"

"We think James has been abducted. We're going to his house."

"Oh, no!" Skauty said. "Any word from Viviana?"

"I got a message on my phone that four have been taken. I assume that includes her," Sam said.

"I wish she hadn't gone off on her own," Skauty moaned.

"Me, too," Sam said as sadness washed over his soul. "I've been thinking I should resign as clan leader. That might put an end to all of this."

"No," Skauty said firmly. "If Tlingit people are doing this they need to be brought to justice. Resigning just lets them win."

"I thought you would say that. Do you want to come with us?"

"I haven't had my coffee yet, so I think I'll stay here."

Sam took his heavy heart and followed Evie to the car.

Joe came right behind. "We had better take two cars, just in case."

They arrived at Tamara and Jame's home. Everything looked in order. The old stone home had been Tamara's grandparents' house. Evie tested the door. It was unlocked. She called out, "James! James!" and ran from room to room.

Joe came in. "The car is in the garage. No signs of a struggle," he observed.

"James wouldn't have gone without a fight unless the guy had a gun aimed at him," Evie said.

"I imagine that's exactly what happened," Joe said as he donned a glove and picked up a nine by twelve envelope from the couch. "I wonder if the abductor disguised himself and pretended to be delivering this letter." He put the letter back and took a photo.

Sam noticed a piece of paper on the dining room table. He leaned over and read.

"Yes I see
Observation
Unlocks the mystery.

Where one seeks
Illumination
Likely will find
Lingering dread.

Does one push
Irreverently on
Every door?"

"What is it, Sam?" Evie asked as she walked over.

"It's a weird poem," he said. "It sounds like a warning."

Joe leaned over with Evie to read. "That's strange," he said and took a photo. "Not that it will do any good, but I'm going to get my equipment and dust for prints.

Sam's gut knotted up. He had a feeling the poem was directed at him. Then anger began to rise. "Of course I'm going to push on every door. I'm going to do everything I can to find you!" he said, clenching his fists.

A car stopped outside, and Sam tensed even more. A moment later, Bryant hurried through the door. "I got here as quickly as I could. What have you found?"

"There is an envelope that looks like it might have been hand delivered. Then there is an odd poem," Joe answered.

Bryant read the poem and knotted his brow. "I don't think we can hope he is just out for a jog."

Sam jumped when something brushed against his leg. He looked down to see Tamara's long-haired calico cat. "Hey, Patches." He leaned down and picked her up. Patches nuzzled his chin and said, "Meow."

"At least you're OK," Evie said, coming over to pet her. "Oh, no! We have to tell Tamara! What if he is after her, too?"

"I'll call her," Sam said.

"No, you can't call her! This is going to be too painful to hear over the phone."

"You're right. Joe, is there anything else you need from us? If not, we'll go to Tamara's office and tell her the bad news," Sam said.

"We don't need anything from you, but I don't think it's a good idea for you to go unprotected," Bryant answered.

"I'll go then," Evie said and started for the door.

"Oh, no, you don't," Sam said. "I'm coming with you."

"I'd rather you wait till we process this crime scene. Then one of us can go with you," Joe requested.

"I don't think I can stand to wait that long," Evie said. "We'll drive straight to Tamara's office and bring her back here."

Sam put Patches down, and she trotted over to her food dish. "Evie's right. We'll be OK." He took Evie's arm and headed for the door, not waiting for an answer.

Joe started to protest but could tell Sam had made up his mind. "No stops in between, please." Joe followed them out and brought back his equipment. He started with the envelope and poem.

"When you finish dusting, you need to go home and get some sleep. I'll take over with the Hansons," Bryant said.

"Thanks," Joe responded.

"Any word on Sandi Aspen?"

"No calls have come in."

Bryant took the poem from Joe and studied it. After a few minutes, Joe heard, "Oh dear."

"What is it?"

"The poem is an acrostic. Look at the first letter of each line."

"Oh no! This just took a turn for the worse."

Chapter 12

Viviana could hear her name being called somewhere down a dark tunnel. It sounded like David's voice. She wanted to get to him but couldn't move. Something was moving her arm and patting her hand. David's voice was closer. She was finally able to open her eyes, but there was only darkness. She could sense the pleading urgency in David's voice. It was him moving her arm.

"Viviana! Are you OK?"

Her head hurt. She struggled to consciousness. "Where am I?"

"Thank God!" David said. "I was afraid you were going to die."

Viviana strained to sit up. Her cheek pounded. Memories of what had happened came flooding back. "I think I hit him in the arm with an arrow. I was trying to aim another one when he hit me with a rock. He was so fast that he was on me before I could release. That's all I remember."

"We heard. He said he would kill us if we called out to you."

"We?"

"Sandi is here, too."

"We're in the shack," Viviana said, remembering the man hiding behind it. "Is this a sleeping bag?"

"He left us sleeping bags to help keep warm."

"He's such a considerate creep," Sandi said.

"Is he gone?" Viviana asked.

"I think so. He dragged you in and left. He had some choice words about your shooting him."

"Let's go then," Viviana said and started to stand up. It was then that she noticed her ankles were shackled. "What is this?" She flicked the sleeping bag open and felt.

"He has us tied to a cable," David explained. "There is enough length to get to the latrine outside.

"That's clever," Viviana said. "I guess he doesn't like foul odors. I'm sure there is nothing here we can use to cut ourselves loose."

"We haven't found anything," David said. "How did you find us?"

"Canto led me to the house. Then I was able to follow the trail. I was lucky that it snowed."

"You call this lucky? Let's get you zipped up into that sleeping bag before you get too cold."

* * *

Sam and Evie pulled up to Tamara's office.

"She's not going to take this well," Sam said.

"I wouldn't either, so don't get yourself abducted," Evie said.

They walked into the office and were greeted by the secretary.

"We need to speak with Tamara," Sam said.

"Do you have an appointment?"

"No, but this is urgent."

"I'll be happy to make you an appointment."

"Good grief!" Evie huffed and knocked on Tamara's door.

"I'm afraid I have to ask you to leave," the secretary demanded as Tamara opened the door.

"Hey, Evie... Sam," Tamara said with a puzzled look. "Come in."

"I'm afraid we have bad news," Sam said, not beating around the bush. "James was abducted this morning."

Tamara's face froze in shock. She stumbled to her desk and sat down. "I told him to be careful," she mumbled. "What am I going to do?"

"Right now, we're going to take you home," Evie said. "Then you're coming to our house where there will be police protection."

Tamara's tears began to flow. "I don't know if I can take this."

Sam's heart went out to her. Evie put her hand on Tamara's shoulder. "Let's get your purse and go."

"I have to have my computer, too. And this note pad." Tamara was stuffing things into a leather bag but suddenly stopped. "I just got James. I can't live if I lose him now."

Evie hugged her. "We'll just have to get him back then."

* * *

"I got some prints off the envelope," Joe said.

"I'll bet there is a ninety-nine point nine percent chance that they are the victim's," Bryant said.

"I'm sure you're right. Do you want to split up and see if the neighbors saw anything?"

"Sure. Which way do you want to go?"

After knocking on doors up and down the street, Joe and Bryant met back at Tamara's house.

"Anything?" Bryant asked.

"I woke up one older lady. She didn't hear or see anything. I guess the rest of these folks are at work."

"I got nobody. The house two doors down has a security camera, though. We could check to see if it picked up anything."

"Tamara will probably know who lives there."

Tamara's car pulled into the driveway. Evie was driving. Tamara walked in without a word.

"I'm sorry," Joe said. She didn't respond. Patches rubbed against her leg. She picked her up and hugged her close. She put Patches down, and the cat stayed right with her. Tamara sat on the couch, and Patches nestled next to her, as if trying to comfort her.

"I'm so sorry, Tamara," Bryant said. "We're doing everything we can to catch this guy. There is a security camera on the house two doors down from yours. It might have picked up something. Can you tell me who lives there?"

"Janelle Standridge. She works at the fish factory."

"Thanks. Joe, can you get your other officer to go by the factory?"

"Of course," Joe answered and made the call on his radio.

"You need to go home and get some sleep," Bryant said. I'll take the prints and get them run."

"I won't argue with that." Joe gathered his equipment and paused when he got to Tamara. "Again, I'm sorry, Tamara. That seems such a trite thing to say, but it's all I've got."

"Thanks, Joe," Tamara said.

After Joe left, Sam looked up to see Bryant pacing back and forth in the dining room, left arm across his chest holding the right elbow and right hand gripping his jaw.

Feeling concerned, Sam asked, "Are you in pain?" Bryant didn't seem to hear him, so Sam decided he was deep in thought.

After a couple of minutes, Bryant suddenly responded. "Sorry, I was trying to process what we have so far. The perpetrator has abducted one person every day. Yesterday, there were possibly two people taken, but that could have been because Viviana found him.

"I think his plan is to take one person a day until he gets everyone he wants. If the email you got is right, then there is one more person he plans to take. Would that be you, or someone else and then you? I don't know. If it's someone else, who do you think it would be?"

Bryant stopped, and Sam realized he actually wanted an answer. Sam tried to process the possibilities. "If this is a disgruntled Tlingit, then he has everyone who was adopted into the clan and connected to me."

"Except for me. I think I'm next." Evie announced.

Sam's chest tightened, and he struggled to breathe. He didn't want to accept the thought but knew Evie was right. "And if it is related to MC2 and GFS, then Evie or Tamara would likely be the next targets. They were both involved in the battle against Harrison."

"I think this is more likely Tlingit related. The parts of the poem about seeking illumination and knocking irreverently indicate a religious or racial dimension to the perpetrator's thoughts. Sam, can you think of anyone in the clan who really resented you becoming clan leader?"

"There were a lot of people who didn't like me when I was growing up. I was bullied a lot because of being mixed race."

"Does any one of them stand out?"

"George Jansen was probably the worst."

"He's the one you said spoke out at the meeting?"

"Yes."

Bryant wrote on his note pad and resumed pacing. "What did the officer find out about George Jansen?" Bryant asked while pulling out his phone. Sam decided he was talking to himself since he called Joe without looking up.

"Hey, Joe. I have a quick question before you go to bed. What did the officer find out when he interviewed George Jansen?... I see. Because of the language of the poem, I'm leaning toward this being a Tlingit matter. But we'll talk more after you've rested. Thanks. I won't bother you again." Bryant pocketed his phone and resumed pacing.

"Well?" Evie asked.

Bryant stopped, and the look on his face made Sam think he had forgotten anyone was in the room with him. "Oh, Joe said that no one was home. The officer hasn't been able to find Jansen yet."

"I need to do some snooping on my computer," Sam said. "Besides, I think we have left Mom and Grandpa alone long enough. Let's go back home, Evie."

"Tamara, I think you need to come and stay with us," Evie said.

Tamara said, "I want to be here if James comes back. Besides, I can't leave Patches."

"Oh boy," Bryant said, running his fingers through his hair. He paced a little harder.

Sam looked at Evie to see if she understood. She shrugged her shoulders and asked, "What is it, Bryant?"

"I think I need to stay with you and Sam since you seem to be the most likely targets. It would make my life easier if you would agree to go to the Hansons' house, Tamara."

"We can bring Patches," Evie added.

Patches chimed in with a meow.

"OK. Patches thinks that's a good idea. I'll have to gather up her food and litter box."

"Good. I'm going on to the house to check on Mom and Grandpa. I hope they're OK." Sam took off without waiting for Bryant's objection.

Chapter 13

The Tesla parked itself in the garage, and Sam rushed into the house. Sandra and Skauty were sitting at the kitchen table drinking coffee.

"Why are you in such a rush?" Sandra asked.

"I was worried something might have happened to you while we were gone."

Skauty nodded toward the cabinet next to which he had parked his shotgun. "We're safe and sound."

"Did you find James?" Sandra asked.

"No," Sam sighed. "I have to get into MC2's and GFS's systems to see if I can find any communication about this." He poured a cup of coffee and started up the stairs. "Oh, Evie is bringing Tamara and her cat in a little bit."

Sam started with GFS and found that they had patched the way he got in last time. He switched to MC2 and was able to get into the system quickly. Sam went straight to Mitch Carter's emails. There were hundreds. "How am I going to look through all of these?"

He decided to scroll through the inbox and look for anything from Holmes Harrison. Sam realized that he was scrolling too quickly. He took a deep breath to quell the panic, went back to the beginning, and made himself slow down.

Finding one from Harrison, Sam opened it. He was disappointed to see it was a congratulation for Carter's getting the go-ahead to expand his operations into Mexico. He found several emails about Mexico but nothing about the abductions. Sam switched to the sent folder. There was nothing of interest there, either.

It was lunch time when Sam came back down. Evie and Sandra were preparing sandwiches. Tamara sat silently, holding Patches.

"Did you find anything?" Evie asked.

"Nothing."

"That's not surprising," Bryant remarked as he came in from the den.

Bryant didn't elaborate, so Sam asked, "Why do you say that?"

"When people are plotting something illegal, they won't communicate in a way that leaves a trail. Unless they're really dumb, and I don't think members of the A-30 could be categorized as dumb. They wouldn't even use texts. It would all be done by phone conversations. That is, unless they create a code language to use."

"I guess I should have thought of that," Sam said, hanging his head. "I did find some talk about expanding operations into Mexico. Do you think that could be code for what's happening?"

"I doubt it, but we could check to see if an expansion is planned."

"I wish I had thought of that. How could I find out?"

"I'm afraid that's beyond my pay grade," Bryant answered.

* * *

Night fell, and Viviana worked out of her sleeping bag to go to the latrine. Heavy snow made it harder to find. "It's snowing like crazy," she said stepping back into the shack.

"It snows a lot more in these higher elevations," Sandi said.

Rey sounded an alarm. Canto joined in, too.

"He's coming," Viviana said. "Let's get on each side of the door and overpower him when he comes in." Viviana hurried to the wall beside the door and David positioned himself on the other side.

"I don't know that this is a good idea," David whispered. "He has a taser and a gun."

"If we can get him on the ground with this cable around his neck, those won't matter."

"What if he doesn't have the key on him?"

"We're going to die, anyway. We might as well take him with us," Viviana said.

"That's not very hopeful," David lamented.

"Shhh," Viviana hissed.

Waiting in the darkness, time seemed to stop. Viviana looped the cable in her hand. She planned a kick to the knee, then strangling him with the cable. They waited, and the birds continued their warning calls.

The door opened and a bright light flooded the shack. Viviana tensed, ready to attack.

"Throw out one of the shackles," the man called. When nothing happened, he said, "If you value your friend's life, you will do as I ask."

"What if this isn't a friend of ours?" Viviana responded.

"Suit yourself."

"Wait, don't!" Viviana heard James' distressed plea.

"We're getting the shackle," she said.

"Don't come out. Just toss it out the door."

Viviana did as she was told.

"On the ground," the man ordered.

Viviana heard the smack of flesh against flesh, and a scuffle ensued. She shuffled out as fast as her shackled ankles would allow. James screamed and fell to the ground. The giant leaped to her and pushed a taser into her ribs. She crumpled.

"Anybody else?" he taunted.

David could see James was moving. The man hurried to him. Snow was already covering Viviana. David started out the door, and the man yelled, "Are you sure you want to do that!" David froze, and the man finished locking the shackles onto James.

"If you want them to live, you can drag them inside," he said, and walked off into the snow.

David rushed to Viviana and scooped up her limp body.

Chapter 14

A knock on the door startled Sam. The long twilight had set in, and it was hard to see who was there.

"Wait. Let me open it," Bryant said as he pulled out his gun.

"It's Joe," sounded from the other side.

Bryant opened the door and welcomed him in. "I hope you got some sleep," he said.

"Slept like a baby," Joe said. "Did I miss any new developments?"

"Sam looked into emails at MC2 but didn't find anything related to the case, which is not surprising. How did you do that, anyway?" he asked Sam.

"You probably don't want to know," Sam said.

"That's what I suspected. Do you think you could do something similar with George Jansen? It would help us determine if he is involved."

Sam lit up at the idea. "I would have to figure out his email address and where the account is hosted."

"His email address should be listed in the Tlingit app," Skauty said. "We keep people's information under 'Contacts.'"

"I just can't imagine George doing this," Joe said. "I'm sure he wouldn't have the skills to pull off leaving no evidence at the scenes."

"That's probably true. But we might find evidence that he is involved with hiring someone with the skills to do that," Bryant pointed out. "Oh, have we found George yet?"

"I checked with Hank and Wendy on my way over. He was still gone when they checked his house last night," Joe answered.

Joe's radio sounded off. "Come in, Joe."

"Hey, Hank."

"Sir, we have a problem. I went to the bathroom, and when I came out Stan was gone."

"Did you check outside around the house?"

"Yes. No sign of him."

"How about his car?"

"It's gone."

"Roger that. Hold on just a minute while I discuss this with Bryant."

"Does Stan know we are looking into George Jansen as a potential suspect?"

"I think so," Joe answered.

"Uh-oh. Get Hank to Jansen's place as quickly as you can. And you get there, too." Bryant grabbed his jaw. "This could be a problem. I hope George is still gone." He started to pace.

"Hank, I need you to go to Jansen's house now. Stan may have gone there to confront George."

"Roger that. I'm on my way."

Hank parked in front of Jansens' house. Stan's car was in the driveway. As he hurried to the door, he heard shouting. Through the front window, he saw Stan waving a pistol. Hank started to storm in, then decided it would be better to knock.

Sarah Jansen opened the door looking terrified. "Am I glad to see you!"

Hank left his weapon holstered. "Hey, George. Stan." He could see rage flashing in Stan's eyes. "Would you mind putting the gun down, Stan?"

Stan glared at him, breathing hard. He started to tuck the gun into his waistband.

"Actually, I'd rather you hand it to me," Hank said.

Stan tossed it on the couch, and Hank picked it up.

"Do you mind telling me what is going on here?" Hank asked.

"He came storming in here accusing me of kidnapping Sandra!" George yelled. "I would never do anything like that! I consider them my friends. Or at least I used to." He glared at Stan.

"You were mad that Sam became clan leader, and Sandi stood up to you about that at the meeting."

"You're right. I don't think a half-breed has any business being our clan leader. But I wouldn't kidnap Sandi because of that."

"Can you tell me where you were Saturday evening?" Hank asked.

"I was here at the house," George said.

"Actually you weren't here," Sarah spoke up. "You ran to the store to pick up a flush valve for the toilet, remember?"

"Oh yeah. But other than that I was here."

"Do you by any chance have the receipt?" Hank asked.

George threw his hands into the air. "You, too! You actually think I kidnapped my friend!"

"Since the two of you had a disagreement, we are just making sure," Hank said, keeping his voice calm. "The receipt would clear it all up."

"I threw it away," George growled.

"Which hardware store did you buy it from?"

"Horse and Wagon Hardware."

There was a knock on the door.

"What is this? Grand Central Station?" George fumed going to the door.

"Hey, George," Joe said.

"I suppose you are going to arrest me now."

"Do I need to?" Joe asked.

"Great Scott! No! You need to arrest Stan for barging into my house and pulling a gun on me!"

"Let's all calm down," Joe said. "We need to sort this out. Could we have a seat in the living room?"

"My wife is missing, and you want me to sit down and chat?" Stan barked.

"You're right, Stan. What we really need is for you to go back home in case there is a call," Joe said.

"I'm tired of being a prisoner in my own home. I'm tired of waiting. It's time to do something!"

"I can't imagine how hard this is, Stan. We are doing all we can to locate Sandi. You may not know that three others have also been abducted. We are working to find all of them and trying to figure out where the perpetrator will strike next. The best thing you can do to help is go home and stay there," Joe explained.

Hank stood in silence watching Joe try to manage Stan's rage. He wondered about George's alibi on the night Sandi was abducted. He wrote a note to check with the hardware store.

"Can I at least go by the store and do some work?" Stan asked.

"I think that's a good idea if you feel up to it," Joe said. "Hank will stay with you."

"I'm tired of being babysat, too," Stan said and stormed out the door.

"George said he had gone to the hardware store at the time Sandi was abducted," Hank told Joe as he hurried out to follow Stan.

"Hank, get Stan to have calls forwarded from the house to his cell phone. Take good notes if anyone calls."

"Roger that," Hank called as he hopped into his car.

* * *

For the second night in a row, David feared for Viviana's life. His heart raced as he scooped her limp body out of the snow. David pulled open the door to the shack. Rey and Canto flew in.

David eased Viviana down and zipped her into the sleeping bag. She was breathing. He put his ear to her chest and could hear her heart beating. He hurried back out to James.

Kat, the kestrel, had landed beside James, who was easing up on one elbow. David helped him to his feet and into the shack.

"What is with these birds?" Sandi said from the corner to which she had scooted.

"These are our friends," David said. "They have helped us through a lot of crises."

Rey was pulling at Viviana's hair. She swatted, and he flew out of the way. Then he flew right back and tugged again. David pulled out a sleeping bag and handed it to James. "Use this to keep warm. It feels like there is one more left. I wonder whom that is for."

David knelt by Viviana and gently shook her shoulders. "Wake up, please," he pleaded. She squirmed and punched at David. He moved quickly enough that her fist glanced off his arm. "Hey, it's me! You're OK."

Rey cawed gently.

Viviana quit fighting and said, "What happened? My ribs sure hurt."

"The monster tased you," David said.

"Now I remember," she said. "I heard James hit the guy, and I tried to go out and help take him down. I saw James fall, then he was on me. That's the last I remember."

"Rey and Kat attacked him after he picked up the shackles," James said. "I tried to seize the opportunity and punched him in the face. He was like a rock. It didn't seem to faze him. I think he hit me with the taser then."

"This guy is too strong to overpower. We are going to need some kind of weapon... Or a trap," Viviana said.

David heard wings fluttering at the door. "I think Rey wants out." He opened the door, and the crow flew into the darkness.

Viviana continued, "Can you think of ideas for a trap?"

"Is that a cable?" James said discovering his ankles weren't only shackled.

"We're on leashes. We have enough run to get to the latrine," David explained.

"We could make a loop with the cable and close it around his feet," Viviana said.

"But what is the chance he would step where the loop is?" James asked.

"What if we all made loops? He might step into one of them," David suggested.

"True. But if he sees all of us outside the shack, I think he will be suspicious," James countered.

"We don't know when he will come, so we might be waiting in the cold a long time," Viviana added.

Rey cawed at the door, and David opened it. "Well, come in," he said when Rey just stood there. Rey picked up something with his beak, and David finally noticed it. "He brought an arrow!" David took it, and Rey flew away. "This might give us a chance against his taser! I don't guess he can carry your bow?" David asked, hoping he was wrong.

Every few minutes, Rey returned with an arrow until he had brought all twelve. Viviana kissed him on the head. "You may have just saved us, mi amigo."

Chapter 15

"**S**o you were at the hardware store Saturday evening around six-thirty," Joe picked up questioning George.

"Are you really going to question me about this?" George snapped.

"George, part of investigating a crime is ruling out any potential suspects. You have an alibi, so we should easily be able to say you weren't involved. But I have to be able to say that with certainty."

"Yes, I was at the hardware store."

"How long were you there?"

"Good grief! Long enough to pick up a toilet valve."

"You were there longer than that," Sarah piped in. "He usually checks out their entire inventory when he's there. I think it was around eight-thirty when you got home."

"So there! I like to browse at the hardware store. Is that a crime?"

"George, I am not accusing you. I just need to know what you were doing at the time of Sandi's abduction. Do you remember the person who checked you out?"

"It was a young lady. I don't know her name."

"Officers came by Sunday and this morning, but you weren't home. Do you mind telling me where you were?"

"We went to visit Sarah's sister down in Port Alexander. We stayed overnight."

Joe looked at Sarah, and she nodded.

"So you were with Sarah's sister the whole time?"

"Yes."

"Well, except while he was out fishing yesterday and this morning," Sarah clarified.

"Who were you fishing with?"

"I borrowed Hal's boat and went by myself. I like being out on the water."

"What did you catch?"

"I'm embarrassed to say, but I caught nothing."

"Two days fishing, and we didn't even get a dinner out of it," Sarah scolded.

"Can I help it if nothing was biting?"

George was clearly still irritated. Joe decided he had enough information to work on corroborating George's story. He wrote a couple of notes in his pad. "Thank you for your time. I hope you have a good evening."

From his car, Joe called Bryant to update him on the interview with George. "I have time to get to Horse and Wagon Hardware before it closes, so I think I'll drop by. Do you need me to stay with the Hansons tonight?"

"No, State Patrol is sending an officer to take the night shift," Bryant answered. "You deserve a night off. Go home after you stop at the hardware store. We'll figure out a way to corroborate George's stay in Port Alexander tomorrow."

"I like that plan," Joe said and hung up.

He pulled into the hardware store at 5:50 pm, ten minutes till closing. He went in and asked, "May I speak with the manager?"

"I guess that would be me since I'm the only one here," the young, dark-haired woman said with a smile.

Reading her name tag, Joe said, "Beth, I need to find out if George Jansen was here Saturday evening about this time.

"I do remember George coming in recently. I think it was Saturday, but I'm not sure."

"He said he bought a flush valve for his toilet."

"I can't say that I remember what he bought. Saturdays are busy. I do remember that he was in and out in a hurry, though. That's unusual for George."

"Is there any way to see if he bought anything Saturday?"

"Let me grab a couple of flush valves, and I can see." She scanned the first valve and did a search for recent purchases. "Nothing on this one."

She did the same with the second valve and studied her monitor. "Yep, here it is." She turned the monitor so Joe could see the record of George's credit card purchase.

"Saturday at five forty-three," Joe said as he wrote in his notepad.

"Do you think Joe abducted Sandi? And the others?" Beth said, her eyes becoming wide.

"I'm not at liberty to say why I'm asking questions," Joe responded automatically. He could tell that Beth took that as a yes.

* * *

A loud thump came from upstairs. Another thump had Bryant on his feet. "Something's happening upstairs!"

Thump.

Bryant was three stairs up before Sam could say, "That's Evie throwing clay."

Bryant slowed down but went up to check, anyway. He found Evie slamming a ball of clay onto the table. "This helps when I'm frustrated," she said.

"I'm just making sure everything is OK. What are you going to make?"

"I don't know. I just felt like pounding something."

Bryant went back downstairs and settled on the couch. Sam was watching the news.

Sam tensed when he heard a car pull into the driveway. He noticed Bryant didn't seem concerned. "Are you expecting someone?"

"Yes. State Patrol is sending an officer to stay with you tonight," Bryant answered. "I suspect that's who this is." He got up and looked out the window. "Yep, it's a patrol car," he said, pulling his weapon. He opened his phone, and Sam could see he was looking at a picture. "We suspect this perpetrator disguises himself. I'm taking no chances," he explained.

Sam flicked on the front porch light. Bryant holstered his gun. "That's him," he said and opened the door.

"Bill Brightwell reporting in," the officer said.

"Bryant Stancil, ABI. Thanks for coming," Bryant responded, stepping aside so the officer could enter. "This is Sam Hanson."

Thump.

"Nice to meet you," Sam said. "I appreciate your willingness to help out."

Thump.

"Glad to be of service," Bill said.

Sam noticed Bill looking at Bryant with raised eyebrows.

Thump.

"That's Sam's wife throwing clay. She said it helps get out her frustrations. I'm sure you'll meet Evie later."

"That explains it. I doubt the perpetrator could enter the second floor without our knowing, though."

"That's true but don't underestimate him. He has abducted four people and left no clues whatsoever," Bryant said. "If you hear anything suspicious, check it out immediately."

"Yes, sir," Bill said.

"Is there anything I can get for you?" Sam asked. "We'll keep a pot of coffee going, of course."

"Thanks. I brought a thermos and some snacks. But I might need to replenish the coffee before the night's over."

"You're welcome to anything we have to eat, too," Sam said. "I'm afraid we've already had supper."

"No problem. I had a burger and fries on my way over."

Sandra stepped out of her bedroom. "I thought I heard voices."

"Bill, this is Sandra, Sam's mother. Sandra, Bill. He will be staying here tonight."

"Thanks for coming. The stress of this has us all on edge. I can't believe it is happening here in Sitka."

Sam could sense his mother's worry.

"I'm happy to be of service, ma'am," Bill said.

"I think it would be wise to do perimeter scans every hour," Bryant said. "It will let the perpetrator know we are watching. Maybe that will serve as a deterrent."

"Yes, sir," Bill answered.

"Sandra sleeps on the first floor. We could put something in front of her window that would alert you in case he tries to come in there."

"Yes, sir. But do you really think he will try anything with me here?"

"I hope not. So far everyone he has taken has been alone. But we think Evie may be the next target. She's the one upstairs throwing clay."

"Wait. Listen," Bill said.

Sam knitted his brow, trying to listen for something suspicious.

"The thumping stopped," Bill explained.

Sam heard what sounded like a window opening. Bill led a charge up the stairs. He flew into the room, gun drawn, with the others close behind. He saw Evie jump, and a bluebird flew and landed on the curtain rod, chirping madly.

"What in the world!" Evie said. She held up her arm, and Azul flew back to her.

Bill looked back at the others, mouth open and eyes wide.

"Another bird?" Bryant asked.

"That is Azul. He's Evie's friend," Sam explained.

"Do you mind explaining this charge of the Light Brigade?" Evie asked, her other hand going to her hip.

"Sorry, ma'am. I noticed you had stopped throwing your clay. Then I heard the window open. Just wanted to make sure you were OK," Bill explained.

"You about scared poor Azul senseless," Evie said.

"Not to mention the rest of us," Tamara said from where she sat on a pallet with Patches and a book.

"Bill, this is Tamara. She is another one of your charges."

"What is all the ruckus?" Skauty asked coming out of his bedroom. "My goodness! We have quite a crowd. I shouldn't have put on my pajamas. Skauty Hanson. I don't believe we have met," he said, extending a hand toward Bill.

"Bill Brightwell, Alaska State Patrol. I have the pleasure of staying with you tonight. I'm afraid I'm also the source of the commotion."

"Nonsense. I am grateful that you do your job so well. It makes me feel safer."

"Thanks," Bill said.

Chapter 16

Evie came flying down the stairs, pulling on her robe. Bill jumped out of the recliner and nearly spilled the coffee on the table next to him.

"Someone's out there!" Evie whispered urgently.

"I haven't heard anyone," Bill said.

"Don't you hear the birds? They're telling us something is wrong."

"Turn out these lights and turn on the outside ones," Bill ordered and moved to the window. He scanned the front yard and just caught sight of a white vehicle pulling away.

"They're gone," Evie said.

"How do you know that?"

"The birds have stopped their alert."

"You're right. I did see a vehicle driving away with no lights on."

"The guy was here. He's after us!" Evie said as the shock sat in. Sam and Tamara came down the stairs.

"What's going on?"

"The guy who has been kidnapping everyone was here! I heard the birds sounding the alarm, and Bill saw him driving away."

"Of course, we don't know that it was the perpetrator," Bill said. "I just saw a car driving with no lights on. It could have been someone that just forgot to turn them on."

Evie gave him a look that made him wish he hadn't said that.

"We're all on the second floor except Mom," Sam said.

Evie bolted to Sandra's bedroom, and the others followed.

"Are you OK?" Evie nearly shouted as she burst through the door.

"What is it?" a sleepy Sandra responded.

Evie leaped onto the bed and grabbed Sandra in a hug.

"It's good to see you, too, Evie. What time is it? Did I oversleep?"

"It's two-thirty," Sam said.

"Are you crying?" Sandra asked.

"The guy was here," Evie managed through her tears. "I was afraid he might have gotten you."

"Honey, we have Bill here. We're going to be OK," Sandra consoled.

"But he was so quiet Bill didn't hear him. The birds sounded the alarm. If it weren't for them, I don't know what would have happened."

"I'm sorry, Evie. I will be more vigilant from now on," Bill said. "He won't sneak up on us again."

"It's not your fault. This creep is apparently very good at what he does," Evie answered.

"I guess that's the end of sleeping for tonight," Sam said. He went to the kitchen and checked his phone. "I'm sorry you're not sleeping. I would tell you who is next, but the plan has to come to fruition. >>>>Solar Wind"

Sam dropped the phone and took a step back. He looked around half expecting to see someone watching him. "That's too creepy," he croaked.

"What's too creepy?" Evie said coming into the kitchen. "Sam, you look like you've seen a ghost."

Sam froze. He wanted to show Evie the message, but he didn't want to frighten her. He didn't want her to feel what he felt right now.

"Sam, what is it?" Evie persisted.

Sam struggled to come up with a lie to avoid telling Evie about the message. He could see in her eyes that he would never succeed. He gave up the battle in his heart and showed her the phone.

"Oh no!" Evie said. "How could he know we are up?"

"It appears he is able to track my phone somehow."

"Or it is from the person who was just here," Evie pointed out.

Sam couldn't believe what was going on. His nerves tingled in high alert.

"I feel like a fish in a bowl just waiting to be snatched," Evie said.

* * *

Hector drove the electric Hummer silently past the Hansons' house. Lights off. Brooding. A State Patrol car was parked conspicuously in the driveway.

"This one will be tricky. Those blasted birds will make it harder. At least I figured out which bedroom they are in. What to do? What to do?"

He turned around, drove to the house at the end of Indian River Road, and parked the Hummer in the garage. He moved quietly into the house, pureed some broccoli, and added it to a protein drink. He set the drink on the table and thought.

"My extraction is set for Thursday at five pm. I have never failed to finish a job on time. It won't happen this time, either." He looked at the drink with its abrasive green color, then chugged a third of it.

Staring into space, he thought of options as he rubbed the stitches he had put in to close the wound from Viviana's arrow.

"The most efficient way would be to take the house and haul away the targets. The boss wanted as little collateral damage as possible, though.

"Option two: Use the taser to incapacitate everyone and take the targets.

"Option three: Go in and out the bedroom window.

"All of the options require that I take the rest of the targets at the same time. That's not how the boss wanted it, though. It was to be one at a time so the last would suffer the most.

"What to do? What to do? Of course, the boss would never know if I took the last two targets at the same time. I wouldn't tell him," he thought with a smile.

"No. I have my reputation to consider. Hector Hoffman does the job exactly as ordered. If I can get the next target out the window, they will increase security. That might create more collateral damage. The boss didn't say which he would prefer if I had to choose between collateral damage and timing of the targets."

He drank the next third of his concoction.

"The boss will be watching the news. He will hear if there are one or two taken tomorrow.

"Obstacles. I need to identify the obstacles. Number one is the birds. They are too loud. I doubt it was a coincidence that they sounded off during my surveillance of the property. I don't consider them collateral damage.

"Number two is the officer. I don't want to have to kill a law enforcement official. He really has nothing to do with this and is just doing his job. But he won't hesitate to kill me. He can be managed.

"Number three is separating the last two targets. That may be the most difficult. They seem to be aware of whom I'm after. What to do? What to do?

"Start with obstacle number one." He smiled for the second time that night. "The birds should be easy." He drank the rest of his drink and pulled out peanut butter and the sunflower seeds on which he loved to snack. He molded the peanut butter into a ball then poured out the sunflower seeds.

He went to his bag and found the bottle of sodium cyanide he had brought just in case. Donning two pair of nitrile gloves and one pair of rubber gloves, he rubbed the cyanide into the peanut butter. He wet the sunflower seeds and coated them with cyanide. He carefully and thoroughly covered the peanut butter ball with the sunflower seeds. He admired his work a moment then gingerly placed the ball into a plastic container. Carefully removing the gloves, he tossed them into the trash.

Donning two more pair of nitrile gloves, he held up the container. "Obstacle one neutralized."

* * *

At 4:40am Evie finally felt sleepy. "I'm going to try to sleep a little," she announced as she stood from the couch. Sam didn't wake up. Evie turned on the bedroom light long enough to disrobe. She checked the window to make sure it was locked before turning out the light.

Lying down, she tried to picture herself walking on the beach, listening to the crash of waves. She relaxed and drifted off to sleep. She dreamed she was in a haunted house. She ran upstairs to hide from a menace she couldn't see. She stepped into a closet and closed the door. She could hear doors with squeaky hinges opening and closing all over the house. They were getting closer and closer. The piercing screech of the doors dragged her out of her sleep.

When she was finally awake enough, she realized she was hearing Nadashée's call. She bolted upright in bed just in time to hear a crash right outside her window. A loud scrape followed, then another crash on the ground.

Evie jumped up and ran downstairs. Bill was racing out the front door. Sam sat up on the couch. "What is it?"

"I think the creep was trying to get in through the bedroom window."

Evie grabbed her coat, and Sam grabbed the pistol. They followed Bill outside and around the house. Dawn had barely begun to illuminate the world. They found Bill shining his flashlight into the woods behind the house. A ladder lay on the ground under the bedroom window.

Evie leaned into Sam. "I'm scared. If Nadashée hadn't attacked, I would be gone." Sam tried to comfort her with an embrace.

"Get back in the house!" Bill ordered.

Evie's feet seemed frozen to the ground as she surveyed the ladder. Nadashée called from the top of a hemlock. "Thank you, Nadashée."

Sam pulled Evie toward the house. "Wait, Sam," Evie stopped.
"What is it?"

"Don't you hear?"

"I don't hear anything."

"Exactly! Where are Azul and Wingston?" She ran toward the front yard, looking up at the tree where they liked to perch. Then she saw them lying still next to a ball of food.

"No!" Evie screamed and ran to the birds. She scooped up Azul's lifeless body. He was so light in her hands.

"No! No! No!" Evie burst into tears and ran into the house with Azul. Sam picked up Wingston and followed.

Chapter 17

"**S**tupid! Stupid! Stupid! Eagles don't eat seeds," Hector scolded himself as he wrapped his right wrist with an Ace wrap.

"I'm lucky it's not broken. I'm lucky I'm left handed. I may be lucky, but I'm stupid. Stupid! Stupid! Stupid!" He pounded his left hand on the table. "I don't think hauling someone out the window is an option now. The likelihood of collateral damage has risen."

He ate an energy bar and swallowed five ibuprofen. He set the alarm for 9:00am and stretched out on the bed. "I need sleep, even if it is just two hours. Daylight will make it more difficult. Maybe a plan will come to me.

"Wait, I'm still a day ahead of schedule. Relax."

* * *

"State Patrol is providing officers to guard the Hansons around the clock," Bryant said. "That will free us up to investigate." He had met Joe at his office at 8:00am.

"How can this guy take people and just disappear?" Joe asked, rubbing his hands on his thighs as he sat behind the desk.

"He must be hiding them in a remote location," Bryant responded. "Any ideas where that might be?"

"There is not much outside of Sitka proper except a few hunting lodges. Do you think there is much chance that they are still alive?"

Bryant could see the worry on Joe's face and the anxiety in the way he kept rubbing his thighs. He considered his answer carefully. "I think they most likely are still alive. This criminal seems to be gathering his victims for a mass killing. I think he wants Sam to suffer. Unfortunately, he will probably make him watch as the others die."

"In other words, we have to break this case before he gets Sam," Joe said as he resumed rubbing his thighs.

"Let's review what we know so far," Bryant said.

"Could we keep Sam and his family in the jail till we catch this guy?"

"That's a good idea. I doubt they will go for the jail, but we could find a place to hide them so the perpetrator can't find them. Do you know any places?"

"Hmm," Joe thought. He startled when his phone rang. "Joe Ford, Chief of Police... We'll be right there."

"What is it?"

"There was an attempted break-in at the Hansons'. The guy was trying to get in through an upstairs window. Let's go."

Daylight had arrived, but the sun was still behind the mountain as Joe drove up to the Hansons' house. Bill met them outside. Getting out of the car, Joe noticed three dead birds in the front yard.

"What's with the dead birds?" Joe asked.

"It appears the perpetrator put out a poison food ball," Bill answered, pointing toward it. "They were really upset about two of the birds that died."

"Let's get that picked up before we have any more casualties," Joe said.

"About two-thirty this morning, Evie came running down the stairs and said the birds were telling her someone was out there. I did see a white Hummer drive off," Bill explained.

"That's consistent with the vehicle Sam saw at the grocery store," Joe noted.

"About six thirty the eagle screeched. Then I heard a scrape and a crash. I ran out and found a ladder around this side," Bill said and directed Joe and Bryant to where the ladder lay. "It is below the bedroom window where Evie was sleeping."

"I'm guessing you didn't see anyone," Bryant stated.

"No. It was dark. I didn't see or hear anyone. No sign of the Hummer, either."

"Why would a skilled assassin fall off a ladder?" Joe mused.

"Evie thinks the eagle attacked him and knocked him over. They call the eagle, Nadashée," Bill answered.

"I'm beginning to believe this business about the birds," Bryant said.

Bill pointed to the hemlock. "There she is."

"We need a plan to protect these people and catch the perpetrator," Joe said. "Let's go inside."

"Thanks, Nadashée," Joe said as they walked to the door.

Bill poured a round of coffee as Joe and Bryant sat down at the kitchen table. When they heard the garage door open, Bill rushed outside. Joe and Bryant scrambled to follow. They met Sam and Evie. Sam had a shovel, and Evie held Azul and Wingston.

"We're going to bury our friends," Evie said.

"I don't think being out in the open is a good idea," Bryant said.

"I'll stay with them," Bill offered.

Bryant started to protest, but the look on Evie's face made him rethink. "OK but make it quick."

"Could we bury the others, too?" Joe asked.

Bryant could tell Sam and Evie didn't understand. "There are three other birds that died."

"Sure," Sam said.

Bill donned two pairs of gloves, gathered the food ball in an evidence bag, then carried the other three birds around back to join Sam and Evie.

Bryant and Joe reconvened around their coffee.

"It appears the perpetrator has been watching this place enough to know where Evie sleeps and that the birds can sound an alarm. He could be out there right now watching the burial," Bryant began. "We have to assume that he will know if we move them. But we know what he drives so we can tell if he is following. We need a place to hide them, Joe. You get on finding a place. We need at least two officers on the scene."

"Maybe we can convince Stan to come stay at the new place, and the officer with him can be on guard," Joe offered.

"Great idea! You find a suitable location. I'll get busy checking the hunting lodges to see if there are any suspicious bookings."

"Sounds good. We will need to plan carefully on how to move this crew," Joe said and walked toward the door.

"Where are you going?"

"My computer is in the car. I'll work from here."

The den door opened and Sam, Evie, and Bill walked in. Bryant could see that Sam and Evie had been crying. "I'm sorry about the birds," he said.

"Thanks," Sam and Evie replied together.

"Bill, shouldn't you be off by now?" Bryant asked.

"Soranni had a doctor's appointment. She should be here about ten," Bill explained.

"I see." Bryant walked outside to where Joe was typing on his computer, which sat on the hood of his Charger. "We need to talk."

"OK," Joe said.

"The perpetrator plans to take someone today. His first attempt failed, and he may be injured from the fall.

"But not injured enough to keep him from getting away."

"Right. He may change his M. O."

"In what way?"

"He may have to take out people to get to his target. If he's injured enough, he may resort to explosives and just terminate the last targets in place."

"So we need to get them out of here like now."

"That's the problem," Bryant said, rubbing his temples. "He is probably watching us right now. If he is the hired assassin I suspect, then he has anticipated that we will move the targets. We will be vulnerable on the road."

"You're right. We need a diversion."

"We also need a place that is isolated so we don't risk a lot of innocent lives. There is a female officer coming to relieve Bill at ten." With that Bryant turned and hurried into the house.

"Bill, can you get in touch with the officer coming to relieve you?"

"Yes, sir."

"Please tell her to bring," Bryant stopped and counted on his fingers. "Six extra bullet proof vests. I assume that you have one."

"Mine is in the patrol car."

"Get the message to your partner. It's time to put your vest on."

Chapter 18

Joe couldn't believe his good luck when Soranni walked in.

"Hi. Soranni Wilson. I'm here to take over for Bill," she said, extending her hand.

"You have red hair!" Joe responded. He could see the frustration that crossed Soranni's face. "I'm sorry. I should explain. The person who we believe is the perpetrator's next target has red hair. We need a diversion to get her out of here safely. I couldn't have ordered a better decoy."

"I see. That's comforting. I guess that explains these," she said looking down at the mass of vests in her arms.

"Yes. Just put those down anywhere. Bryant Stancil. ABI. Joe, let's get everyone together and go over the plan."

Joe called Skauty and Tamara to come down. Sam, Evie, and Sandra were already sitting at the table drinking coffee. It was 9:55 am.

"I need everyone to listen carefully to the plan," Bryant began. "At ten thirty, three more state patrol officers will arrive. We are going to have Soranni and Evie and Sam and Bill exchange clothes.

"I'm hoping that if the perpetrator is watching, he will think Soranni is Evie. If he tries to engage, he will encounter two armed officers. Bill will be Evie's passenger. I will be with Sam.

"You will take different routes to get to a site that Joe is still working on. If anyone has an idea for a location, I would be happy to hear it. I assume the perpetrator is watching us, so you will all be wearing bullet-proof vests."

"The Walkers might let us use their rental house. It's a few miles south and is on the water. There's nothing nearby," Sam offered.

"What do you think, Joe?" Bryant asked.

"Other than the fact that it has windows, it is a good location," Joe answered.

"It does have trees around it, which would give the perpetrator cover," Skauty pointed out.

"Does anyone have a better idea?"

"What about the old National Guard building?" Joe asked.

"Is there anything nearby?" Bryant asked.

"There is a marine shop next door. It's pretty close."

"Call the Walkers. We don't have time to wait," Bryant said. "Everyone pack lightly. We need to be ready to move in thirty minutes. Joe, who is on with Stan Aspen?"

"Jordan is there today."

"Get word to her that we are moving everyone, including Stan, to this house."

"What can we do about Stan waiting for a call? We can't have his cell phone on," Joe asked.

"I have the GPS on my phone disabled so it can't be tracked," Sam said.

"Are you sure?"

"Yes."

"OK. Have Stan's phone forwarded to Sam's. We will need all other phones turned off. I need everyone to be ready to hustle out the door at 10:30. We want this to happen so quickly that the perpetrator doesn't have time to analyze what's going on," Bryant finished.

* * *

At 8:43, Hector's eyes flew open and a realization hit. "I would move the targets today." He jumped out of bed, stuffed supplies into a duffle bag, and started out the door.

"Stupid. Stupid. Stupid. I will have to have a car to follow them, and I think they saw the Hummer last night. Enough self-loathing. A quick kick to the ego is sufficient. That's how I learn. Now, it's time to move on to action. I need a plan."

It took only a few seconds for the plan to crystalize in his mind. He called an Uber. "Pick me up at the corner of Yaw and Gill Truitt. I'll be waiting outside."

"I should double check." He looked through the duffle bag, taking inventory. "Energy bars, drinks, pistol, taser, C4, extra ammo, binoculars, handcuffs, rope, chloroform, gauze, flashlight. Wait."

He checked his phone for the weather. "I may need rain gear." He added that to the bag and hurried the quarter mile to his pick-up location. He devoured an energy bar and a protein drink while waiting for the driver.

At the rental car location, Hector used a different fake identity and credit card than he had used to rent the Hummer. After driving off, he decided to take a chance. He saw a house where no one seemed to be home. It was just down from the Hansons'. He backed in and acted as if he went into the front door. Then he crouched down, came back to the car, and lay down on the ground so he could see from underneath.

"At least I'm lying on nice, clean gravel and not mud. This will get uncomfortable after a while. Waiting is so tedious." He pulled binoculars from his bag. "Now let's see what you are up to."

* * *

One by one, people showed up in the den carrying bags. Evie set hers down, and Sam said, "We look good in uniforms."

She grabbed Sam. "I'm worried."

Sam squeezed her tightly. "The police will protect us."

"He's watching us. I know it," Evie said, ignoring Sam's comment. "He's not going to let anything stop him from his mission. I don't want to be in a car without you."

"That worries me, too," Sam said.

"Joe, can Sam and I ride in the same car?" Evie asked.

"I'm afraid that would make the perpetrator's job too easy. We want it to be hard for him to get you. Listen up, everyone. It's ten twenty. Please put on your bullet-proof vests. Is everyone ready?"

Joe watched as somber faces nodded. "OK. When the other officers get here, you will each be escorted to a car. I need you to go quickly and get in as fast as you can. Some of the routes we will be taking are long, so don't be surprised if it takes a while for you to get to the new location. We are trying to throw the perpetrator off so he can't find us.

"Evie, you will be driving Bill's car, and he will be your passenger. Do you know your route?"

"Yes," Evie responded.

"Sam, you will be driving Soranni's car, and Bryant will be your passenger. Have you memorized your route?"

"I have," Sam said.

"The officers that are about to arrive have been briefed. We believe the perpetrator is driving a white Hummer EV3. Keep watch for that vehicle."

Three patrol cars pulled up and parked in various places in the driveway, front yard and road.

"They're here," Joe said.

"OK people. Let's roll," Bryant said.

Everyone picked up their bags and headed for the door. Sam gave Evie one last hug. "We're going to be OK," he said.

Evie hugged him back, found Bill, and followed him to the car.

In less than two minutes all five patrol cars were loaded and gone.

Joe left last with Skauty. "I wonder where he is," Joe said pausing to look around before getting into the car.

"I don't know, but I'm sure he's out there somewhere. I don't see a Hummer," Skauty said.

Nadashée screeched from high in the sky as she circled over a house down the road.

"I think Nadashée is saying he is just down the road."

"Let's drive by and see," Joe said. He turned the car around and headed in the direction Nadashée was circling. Driving slowly, he and Skauty scanned the area carefully.

"I don't see anyone," Skauty said.

"He could have seen us coming and hid."

Evie's hands shook as she steered the patrol car. "I don't like this. Something is going to happen."

"I'm armed and ready. You don't have to worry," Bill said, holding up his pistol. "It will be OK."

"No. It won't."

Chapter 19

Soranni leaned over and extended her hand. "Soranni Wilson." "Jason Adams. Nice to meet you," her driver responded, shaking her hand. "Do you think this guy is likely to attack during the move?"

"I hope not. But he seems aggressive. He tried to break in an upstairs window last night. They say an eagle knocked him off the ladder, or he might have captured another victim."

"Wow!" Jason said. "I guess we had better stay alert."

* * *

Hector's attention was piqued when the state patrol cars pulled up to the Hansons' home. His wrist throbbed as he aimed the binoculars.

"Stupid. Stupid. Stupid," he thought but refused to let the pain distract him. He repositioned himself to be more comfortable. When he aimed the binoculars again, people were rushing out of the house and into the cars. He caught sight of red hair shining brightly in the sun. He noted that she got into car 027.

"Looks like it's time to move," he thought as he slid quietly into his car.

* * *

Jason pulled out in line with the other cars. At Sawmill Creek Boulevard, the first three cars turned left. His route was to turn right and go north up Sawmill Creek to the high school by Monastery Street, then loop back down.

Soranni unhooked her seatbelt and got onto her knees to look out the back window. She pulled her service belt out of the bag, put it on, and unholstered her gun.

"So far, I only see patrol cars and Bryant's rental," she informed Jason. "Wait. A silver Jeep just turned onto Sawmill. I should have brought binoculars."

"Keep an eye on it," Jason said. He started to report it on the radio but remembered Joe had told them not to use the radio in case the perpetrator was monitoring their frequency.

Jason continued up Sawmill Creek and turned right onto Monastery. A few seconds later, the silver Jeep turned behind them.

"It's following us," Soranni said.

"I see it," Jason replied. "I'm staying on our route."

"Wait. It's turning left onto De Groff," Soranni said and relaxed the tension in her muscles.

"I guess that's not our guy, then."

Soranni kept watching for anything suspicious. She never saw the Jeep that came flying out of a side street and rammed into the back door on the driver's side. The collision threw Soranni across the car and on top of Jason. She hit her head on the door and everything went black.

Jason checked Soranni's carotid pulse. "You're alive." He struggled to unhook his seatbelt and gently slid her back into her seat. By the time he got out, the driver of the other car was staggering toward him, whiskey bottle in hand.

"Sorry about that," the muscular blond slurred. "I was trying to get home before my wife noticed I wasn't there."

"Stop right there," Jason ordered, aiming his pistol.

"Oh crap! You're the police. This is just water. Sometimes I have to fill the radiator." The guy stopped and staggered, then fell to the ground.

Jason took note that the vehicle was silver and might be the one they had been watching. He approached carefully, gun drawn. "I think I'll cuff this guy first and ask questions later," he thought.

He paused, watching for any movement. The man appeared to be out cold. He holstered his gun so he could get the cuffs on. Seeing the Ace wrap on the guy's right wrist, he knelt down and grabbed the left arm. As soon as he touched him, he flipped over, taking Jason's left arm with him. Jason twisted with the motion and fell onto the man. The last thing he felt was excruciating pain in his left ribs.

Soranni came to and tried to remember what had happened. "Why does my head hurt?" She touched the crown of her head and found blood. A memory of the crash started to form when she saw a large blond male run around the front of the patrol car.

Soranni reached for her weapon, but it was gone. As she reached for her taser, the door flew open. A meaty hand grabbed her wrist and jerked it away from its target. With one arm, the man dragged her out of the car.

Soranni tried to fight back, but she was too off balance to kick or punch. Finally finding her footing, she aimed a kick at his knee. He deftly dodged it, grabbed her leg, and flipped her onto the ground.

She watched as he looked her over, studying the service belt. "You're not my business. You're an officer."

Soranni watched the rage grow on his face. He punched her in the jaw and everything went black again.

* * *

As planned, Bryant and Sam were the first to arrive at the house. Their host greeted them at the front door.

"Stephen Walker. Welcome to Eagles Landing."

"Bryant Stancil, ABI. Thanks for letting us use your home."

"You are more than welcome. We don't get many renters this time of year anyway. I didn't know how many keys you would need," Stephen said, holding out his hand with four keys.

"That should do nicely. Hopefully, we will catch the perpetrator and be out of here soon."

"No problem. Use it as long as you need to." Stephen turned to leave, and the first patrol car pulled in. Sandra hopped out, grabbed her bag, and hurried into the house. Sam was relieved to see his mom safe.

About every five minutes, another patrol car would pull in, drop off the passenger, and take off.

Bill came in with Evie. Sam grabbed her in a hug. "You made it."

"But I still think something's going to happen," she said.

Bill looked Sam over and said, "I think these clothes fit you better than me."

"Yeah, but I do make this uniform look good."

"We might be able to find a position for you on the force. But in the meantime, I need my uniform back." He and Sam changed clothes.

"Anything else you need from me?" Bill said, checking in with Joe before he left.

"No but thank you for staying and helping with this."

"No problem. I'm glad we got here without incident."

Bryant started checking his watch every few seconds. When he started pacing, Sam asked, "What's wrong?"

"Jason and Soranni should have been here by now. They are five minutes late."

"It could be traffic. Or even traffic lights. They might have caught all of them," Skauty said.

"OK. Let's give them another five minutes," Bryant said.

Each second seemed like a minute. Sam noticed that Joe was fidgety. Then he noticed that he was pacing, too.

"I knew something would happen. They've been attacked," Evie said.

Sam could sense the worry in her voice. He also could sense that she was right. Four minutes had passed.

"We need to do something," Sam said. "I'm sure Evie is right."

"Do you want me to drive their route?" Joe asked.

"I think that's a good idea," Bryant said.

"I'll wait till you find out what happened," Bill offered.

"Thanks," Joe said. He checked the map on which he had drawn out the routes and took off. It wasn't long before he saw the crashed patrol car. Jason was sprawled on the ground. Joe screeched to a stop and called for an ambulance.

With dread surging, Joe shook Jason's shoulder. Then he checked for a pulse. "Come on Jason! Wake up! Soranni!"

Joe ran to the passenger side and found Soranni down, too. A bruise bloomed on the left side of her face. He shook her by the shoulder. "Soranni!"

Her eyes opened, and she jumped to her feet, ready to fight.

"It's Joe, Soranni. It's OK."

"Oh, my head! What happened?"

"I was hoping you could tell me." Joe noticed blood matted in her hair. "You are bleeding."

Soranni touched the crown of her head and saw blood on her fingers. "I think we were in a crash."

"Looking at the car, I would say you are right."

"Where's Jason?"

"He's alive but unconscious on the other side of the car."

"Who's unconscious?"

Joe looked to see Jason leaning on the trunk of the car. "Thank God! You had me worried. I think we need two ambulances." Joe made the call. "Jason, do you remember what happened?"

"I assume it was the perpetrator who shot out of the side street and rammed us. He was acting like a drunk who passed out. When I tried to cuff him, I think he tased me. That's the last I remember."

"Now I remember," Soranni said. I saw him walk around the front of the car. I looked for my gun but had lost it in the crash. When I reached for my taser, he picked me up by one arm. I thought my shoulder was going to come out of the socket. I tried to kick his knee, but he threw me to the ground. I think he realized I wasn't Evie and hit me."

The first ambulance pulled up.

"I think I'm OK," Jason said. "I don't need to go to the ER."

"You were injured in the line of duty. It's a requirement. But I think we need to send Soranni first. She may have a concussion," Joe replied.

The second ambulance arrived while the EMTs were still tending to Soranni. A wrecker pulled up as well. In all the chaos, no one noticed the huge blond man attach something under Joe's car.

Chapter 20

Joe parked his car in the garage at the Eagles Landing house so it wouldn't draw attention if the perpetrator drove by.

"Soranni may have a concussion. Jason was tased. They are both at the emergency room getting checked out. Neither will be able to work today," Joe explained to Bryant and the others.

"I'll be happy to stay," Bill offered.

"You have been on too long already," Joe said. "Go home and get some sleep. I'm sure we will need you later, and I want you fresh and alert."

"I can do that," Bill replied and gathered his things to leave.

"Did they say what kind of car rammed them?" Bryant asked.

"A silver Jeep Gladiator," Joe said.

"So the perpetrator has changed vehicles."

"The man Jason and Soranni described matches Sam's description of the one he saw with the white Hummer at the grocery store," Joe said.

"At least he didn't kill anyone," Bryant said. "The fact that he left them alive says he is confident we can't catch him. We are definitely dealing with a formidable foe."

"We have to prove him wrong," Sam said. "That monster has my friends, and I want them back alive."

"We're doing everything we can to find them," Joe said.

"It doesn't feel like we are doing anything but hiding," Evie said.

"I understand your frustration," Bryant answered. "We have an agent checking the rental car places with a description of the perpetrator. We have an APB on the white Hummer.

"That reminds me. Joe, we need an APB out on this new vehicle. Did you say it was a Jeep Gladiator?"

"That's right. I have already called it in," Joe said.

Bryant resumed, "We have increased the number of State Patrol officers in the area, and they are all looking for these vehicles and signs that someone is being held. We are in the process of checking all of the isolated rental cabins.

"That's what Joe means when he says we're doing everything we can. We've devoted more resources to this search every day."

"It's just so frustrating," Evie said.

The front door flew open and Stan stomped in. "This is absurd! I don't see any reason for me to leave my home and hide out here like a rat!"

Wendy followed. "He's not a happy camper."

Joe stepped near the fire place in the large den. "Listen up, everyone. This is hard on everybody. I am sorry that everyone's life has been disrupted. Moving everyone here is our best chance at stopping the abductions while we track down the perpetrator.

"This person appears to be a highly skilled individual who believes he can outwit law enforcement. I suspect he has done that many times in the past. We all have to remain vigilant.

"The forecast calls for a storm to come in around five o'clock this evening. They are saying heavy rain here and up to two feet of snow in the mountains. With the winds, power outages are possible.

"Make sure you have any computers or tablets you need fully charged. Sam, make sure your phone stays charged. Everyone else needs to keep their phones off. Not just on silent but off. If you haven't turned them off yet, do it immediately."

Sam pulled out his phone and rechecked to make sure GPS tracking was disabled. When he opened it, the urgent alert notification was back.

"Moving was clever. It will be time tomorrow morning. Come see me. We can stop these monsters. Tell no one. >>>>>Solar Wind"

Sam froze. "Tell no one" burned into his heart. "I should tell Bryant about this message, but it said not to," ran through his mind. "Bryant said he needed to know any time I got one of these messages. I need to think about this." He closed the screen on his phone and went to his and Evie's bedroom. Pretending to unpack, he tried to decide what to do.

"What's wrong?" Evie asked from the doorway.

"Nothing. I'm just unpacking," Sam tried to lie. He knew it was futile.

"Sam, you know better than to lie to me. Something is bothering you."

Sam's mind fired warnings. "The message said to tell no one. Evie will tell me not to go. I don't want to frighten her." He focused enough to see Evie's eyes and knew he couldn't do it. He had to tell her. "I got another message from Solar Wind. It said that tomorrow morning it will be time for me to come see him, her, whoever this person is."

"That's scary! You're not going anywhere."

"Solar Wind knew that we had moved."

"That's even scarier."

"The message told me to tell no one."

"Bryant and Joe need to know that the perpetrator knows we moved."

"I'm not sure Solar Wind is the perpetrator."

"Why do you say that?"

"He said, 'We can stop these monsters.'" Sam could see that Evie was mulling over what he had said. "I wonder if I should try to find this Solar Wind."

"Has he said where he is?"

"Well, no."

"How would you find him?"

"I suspect he, if this is a man, would send me directions when I start out."

"How would he know you started out?"

"He knew we changed houses."

"That's creepy. Wait, I thought you turned off the GPS on your phone."

"I did."

"Then how did he know we moved. Do you think he is watching us?"

"I have no idea. The same way he knew we were up the other night after the guy tried to break in, I guess."

"It would make sense that the perpetrator would have known that," Evie said. "This Solar Wind may be the perpetrator trying to lure you to him."

"Do you think I should tell Bryant?"

"Yes, I think you should tell him," Evie said, hands going to hips. "He can't help us if he doesn't know what's going on."

"OK," Sam said, knowing there would be no use arguing because Evie was usually right.

Sam handed the phone to Bryant. "I got another message from Solar Wind."

Bryant scrunched his eyebrows as he read over the short message. He kept looking at the phone as if he expected it to explain itself. Finally he handed the phone back to Sam and started pacing.

"Why would he say, 'We can stop these monsters?' Why is monsters plural? We know the perpetrator knows we have moved the targets. Is this the perpetrator or someone else? If it's someone else, that complicates matters."

Sam deduced from Bryant's body language that he was talking to himself, so he didn't respond. Joe had walked into the common room just in time to hear Bryant muttering. Sam noticed the questioning look on Joe's face.

"I got another message from Solar Wind," Sam explained and handed Joe his phone.

"That's not good," Joe said. "I think this is the perpetrator trying to trick you into being captured."

"I agree," Bryant said, surprising Sam that he was paying attention. "He seems to have set a schedule of taking one person a day until he gets to Sam. You would make his life easy by walking into his trap."

"Do you still think he will try to get Evie tonight?" Sam asked.

"Yes. That is why we will have two guards stationed here at all times," Bryant said.

Sam noticed Evie in the corner of his eye and knew she had heard. A heavy weight dragged his heart toward his stomach.

"Hopefully, he won't be able to find us," Joe offered.

Chapter 21

At 5:00pm that Tuesday afternoon, clouds began to roll in and the wind became mischievous, tossing the tops of trees about. Hank turned on the TV to catch the forecast.

"A severe storm is rolling into Sitka right now. We expect heavy rain and wind with gusts up to fifty-five miles an hour over night. The mountains are likely to see up to two feet of snow by morning," the meteorologist said.

"It looks like it's going to be a rough night," Hank said.

Sam agreed and tried to stretch the tense muscles in his neck. "I feel like a sitting duck."

"We've got you covered," Hank said. "Besides, the perpetrator doesn't know where we are."

"I hope you are right," Sam said, not feeling reassured.

"I hope we don't lose power," Skauty said from his recliner.

Sam heard Nadashée's piercing call just outside the kitchen window. He nearly collided with Evie running to see what was up. Peering into the dimming light, he could just see her on a low branch. "I don't see anything but Nadashée."

They heard Skauty call, "Nadashée," and watched her fly around front. By the time they got to the front room, Nadashée was perched on the mantel.

"I let her in during bad weather," Skauty explained.

"That's kind of you," Sam smiled. At the same time, a wave of sadness washed over him. He would never see Wingston again.

Sam was uneasy. He walked to the bedroom and surveyed it. The bed was about two feet from the window. He started working it to the other side of the room. The queen-sized bed was heavy. He moved the foot a couple of inches and then scooted the head. When he had moved the bed a foot, he stood and stretched his back.

Bill, who was back after a short day's rest, poked his head in. "I'm taking orders for supper," he said. "What are you doing?"

" The bed is too close to the window. I want it over here," he said pointing to its intended location. "Then I'm going to slide this chest in front of the window," Sam answered.

"Let me help you with that so you don't pull your back out."

They moved the bed another foot then positioned the chest to block the window.

"Sam, I'm sure you will be safe here. There will be two of us on duty tonight."

"Thanks, Bill. But I don't want to take any chances. It's Evie he is after next."

"I understand. What would you like for supper? We're ordering from Puglisi's."

"I love their chicken alfredo."

"One chicken alfredo on the list," Bill said as he wrote it down.

"I see you have been redecorating," Evie said as she walked into the bedroom. "I like your style."

"I'm worried," Sam said.

"Me, too." Sam and Evie embraced while Bill went to finish collecting the dinner order.

* * *

The wind howled on the mountain, rattling the little shack.

"It's going to be a cold night. I think it will snow hard," Viviana said.

"I sure am hungry. Are you sure he didn't leave anything to eat?" Sandi said.

"I haven't found anything," David answered.

They heard Kat's call at the door. James scooted over in his sleeping bag and pushed it open. The little kestrel hopped in with something in its talon.

"What have you got there?" James said, barely able to see the bird. "He brought us a mouse!"

"Thanks, Kat. But you really shouldn't have," David said from where he and Viviana sat huddled together."

"If it snows, at least we will be able to get water," Viviana said.

"I wish our host was more into creaturely comforts," David said.

"If anyone needs to use the bathroom, I'd go now," Viviana said. "I think the storm is going to get bad.

James worked out of his sleeping bag and made a latrine run. When he came back he said, "It's snowing."

* * *

Around 9:30, the storm got serious. The wind howled and rain came in torrents.

"I'm glad you thought to bring Nadashée in," Evie said. "I would have done the same for Azul and Wingston. I wish they were here."

"Actually, Nadashée was the one who had the idea to come in," Sam quipped from where he and Evie sat on the couch.

Skauty laughed. "You're right, but I would have thought of it sooner or later."

A few minutes later, Sam felt Evie's head land on his shoulder. Tipping over awoke her, and she stretched.

"We didn't get much sleep last night, and it has been a long day. Why don't we go on to bed?" Sam suggested.

"Good idea. I can't seem to hold my head up anyway."

After the bedtime rituals of brushing teeth and getting ready, Evie assessed the bed situation. "There's only one blanket. Help me look for another one. I think it's going to get cold tonight."

Sam helped her search drawers and closets but found none.

"You can laugh if you want, but I'm sleeping in my coat. I don't want to be cold tonight," Evie said.

Sam was too tired to laugh. He kissed Evie good night and snuggled up to her. In a few minutes he could tell by her breathing that she was asleep.

Sam's mind wouldn't slow down. He kept thinking of ways the perpetrator could get at them. "Is the back door locked? Is the garage door down? I know I locked the bedroom window."

When Sam realized he was tossing and turning, he thought he should get up to keep from waking Evie. He sat on the side of the bed and noticed when the light under the door went dark. An eerie silence fell over the house. "The power must have gone out," he thought and got up to see.

Opening and closing the bedroom door as quietly as he could, Sam slipped out. He heard someone in the front room say, "We should have gotten candles out before the power went out."

It sounded like Hank. To ease his mind, Sam decided he would check the back door to make sure it was locked. Bill was stationed in a chair in the kitchen near the door. He was watching something on his phone.

"Just making sure the door is locked," Sam said as he tested the lock.

"I checked it a few minutes ago, too," Bill said.

Sam walked to the front room and found Hank lighting a candle. Joe, Tamara, and Sandra were there, too. Skauty had gone to bed.

"I thought you were going home, Joe," Sam said.

"I decided to stay. The more, the merrier."

With the power out, the howling of the wind and pounding of the rain intensified.

"This is quite a storm," Sam said. He was fidgety and paced around the room.

"Try to relax," Joe said. We have you covered.

"I know, but it's hard when I know he is after my Evie. I think I'll go check on her."

Sam had started back toward the bedroom when he heard a loud crash, and the house shook. It came from the front. He ran back to the front room to see Hank peering out the front door.

"It looks like a pine blew over and landed on the front porch," Hank reported.

Everyone crowded around the door and windows to look. Sam could just make out a tangled mess of branches hanging down from the roof.

"I'll go check on the damage," Hank said as he pulled on his coat and flipped the hood over his head. He pulled the flashlight from his service belt before zipping the coat.

Sam watched the light as Hank aimed it in different directions. He wanted to go out, too, but didn't want to get soaked in the cold rain.

After a couple of minutes surveying the situation, Hank came back in. "It doesn't look too bad. Probably some shingles damaged, but I don't think anything structural was broken." His coat dripped in rivulets as he pulled it off. He hung the coat by the door and headed for the gas log fire.

"I hope the temperature doesn't drop below freezing," Hank said. "We would really have a mess then."

Sam joined him by the fire. "I'm glad we have this fireplace. It's going to get cold without heat."

"Where is Bill?" Joe asked.

"He probably stayed on his post at the back door," Hank said.

"We need someone to find a way to make coffee. It's going to be a long night," Joe said.

"I'll check in the kitchen to see if they have anything we can use," Sam said.

"Bill, we need to find a way to make coffee. Do you have a flashlight?" Sam asked as he turned on the light on his phone. Bill didn't respond, so Sam aimed the light to where Bill had been sitting earlier. Bill lay sprawled on the floor. Time stopped. Panic surged in Sam's soul. The two seconds he stared at Bill seemed an eternity. Finally Sam's body found the ability to act. "Evie!" he called as he ran to the bedroom.

"Oh no! Oh no! Oh no!" She was gone.

Hank, Joe, and the others ran into the bedroom. Sam was standing frozen in place. Sandra pushed through and embraced her son without a word.

Hank and Joe raced out of the room. "Search outside," Joe ordered. "I'll check on Bill. Someone make sure she is not in the bathroom."

Tamara ran to all three bathrooms. No Evie.

"I have to find her," Sam said and pulled away from his mother. He donned his coat and boots.

"Sam, you can't go out in this," Sandra said.

"I have to find her before it's too late," Sam said. "Wait, what is this?" Sam noticed a piece of paper on the bed. He aimed the light and read.

"Sin and shame
 Undying regret
 Follower of fools
 Forever bound
 Eternity
 Reveals"

Rage collided with terror. Sam had to force himself to breathe.

"I didn't find her," Tamara said, returning from her search. "What is that smell?"

Chapter 22

ector hardly noticed the weight of the unconscious Evie slung over his shoulder. He made his way north through trees and storm. The cold rain stung as the wind drove it into his face. His right wrist throbbed after picking up Evie.

Hector thought of the payoff awaiting him. "It will be worth it," he thought, determined to push through the misery to the end.

He continued north for about a quarter of a mile to the white Hummer. He flopped Evie in the back and zip tied her wrists and feet. He tossed the shoes he had grabbed from her room. "It was thoughtful of you to be wearing your coat."

Climbing into the driver's seat, Hector turned the heat on high and drove into the night.

* * *

Realizing how cold it was outside, Sam pulled off his coat, donned a hoodie, and put the coat back on.

"You can't be thinking of going after her," Tamara said.

Sam glared at her as he put his dad's 9mm Luger in his coat pocket. "Someone has to do something. All the police want to do is sit and wait. I'm going to find her."

Sam stomped out of the room, pulling away as Sandra grabbed his arm. He heard Joe in the kitchen saying, "I have an officer down and need an ambulance." Sam decided to go out the front door. He pushed through the branches of the fallen tree and stopped. "Which way would he have gone?" he thought.

He decided back toward town was the most likely option and followed the downed tree trunk north. Sam saw that the tree had been cut down. "Of course. A diversion."

Realizing how thick the trees were, Sam turned to walk out to the road. The wind was so strong it pushed him along, causing him to have to increase his pace to keep from blowing over. He was just about to the road when he heard, "Police! Don't move! Hands up or I'll shoot!"

Sam was so startled he jumped and turned around.

"I said don't move! Hands up!"

Sam's mind raced, trying to decide whether to pull his gun and fire. Before he could get his hand out of the pocket, someone collided with him from the side, and Sam hit the ground. His breath was knocked out, and before he could breathe, the person flipped him onto his belly. A knee landed on his back and he felt the barrel of a gun to his head.

"When I say don't move, I mean don't move."

Sam recognized Hank's voice. He croaked, "Hank, it's Sam."

Sam was blinded when Hank shined his flashlight in his face.

"What are you doing out here?" Hank asked, moving his knee off Sam's back and helping him up.

"I'm going to look for Evie."

Another flashlight bumped up and down, headed in Sam's direction. "What is it, Hank?" Joe yelled over the wind.

"I thought I had found the perpetrator, but it turned out to be Sam," Hank explained.

Sam tried to brush the leaves and other muck off as he said, "I'm going to find Evie. You can either let me go or come with me."

"Sam, there is something you need to know. Bryant said that this type of crime usually means the perpetrator is collecting victims for a mass assassination. I suspect he plans for you to have to watch the others die."

Sam's heart seemed to stop.

"As long as we can keep you out of his hands, the others are most likely safe. Evie's best chance of survival is for you to stay with us until we find her and the others."

Sam's anger boiled over. "My wife is in the hands of a maniac, and all you want to do is sit in the house and wait! That may work for you, but I have to do something!" He jerked his arm from Hank's grasp and turned toward the street.

"I can't let you go," Joe said.

"Try to stop me."

"I won't risk the lives of five people just so you can try to prove your manhood."

Sam kept walking. Red lights and a siren broke through the night. Sam suddenly felt two hands slip under his arms, and he was being dragged back toward the house.

"Let go of me!" he barked as he tried to twist and turn to get loose.

"Sorry, we can't do that," Joe responded.

They dumped Sam in a chair, and Joe went to check on Bill leaving Hank to watch Sam.

"He's coming to," Tamara said as Joe walked up.

The paramedics rushed in behind Joe and began taking vital signs. Bill sat up and leaned against the counter, still groggy. The paramedic taking his blood pressure leaned in and sniffed. "You were chloroformed."

"Do you remember what happened?" Joe asked.

"I heard something at the door, like someone trying to pick the lock. I went to check, and a large man burst through, grabbed my gun hand, and covered my face with a smelly rag. That's all I remember."

"It looks like you will be just fine. Maybe a little groggy for a while, but fine," the paramedic said.

"It's protocol to have him evaluated, so you will have to transport him to the ER," Joe said.

Bill protested, but Joe said, "There's no arguing this point. You know that, so go crawl into the ambulance."

Bill staggered. One of the paramedics grabbed an arm to steady him as he walked to the front room and put on his coat. Bill looked at Sam. "I'm sorry."

"Thanks," Sam replied. Sam looked at his watch. It was 1:49 in the morning. He went for his computer in the bedroom, and Hank followed right behind.

"Are you going to accompany me to the bathroom, too?" Sam grumped.

"If necessary," Hank said.

Sam took the computer back to the living area and sat near the fireplace. He opened the computer and stared at it. He couldn't focus. Fear and anger fought for primacy. Guilt wedged into the fight, too. "Why didn't I stay with her? I'm such an idiot! I shouldn't have left the room."

Thoughts like these swirled in his mind, derailing any productive assessment of the situation. The storm outside seemed to have moved into Sam's soul. He closed his computer. "I need to maintain the charge."

That was the first logical thought Sam had had since he discovered Evie was gone. "I have to pull myself together and come up with a plan. No one can save Evie sitting here. But what if Joe is right? What if Evie's best chance of survival is my not getting taken?"

Sam began to pull a semblance of focus and reason out of the chaos in his soul. He looked to see Hank and the others sitting quietly, faces somber. It dawned on Sam, "They can't protect me. The monster will take me tomorrow if I stay here. My best chance of staying out of his hands and finding Evie is to leave and go out on my own."

* * *

Hector was amused as Evie struggled to put on her shoes with her wrists zip tied. He was thankful the rain and wind had slackened the last few minutes.

"We're going for a rather long hike. Don't try to get away," he said as he brandished a gun in her face. "It will go better for you if you cooperate."

He pushed Evie out into the cold rain and locked the garage door. Evie bolted when he turned to the door. Hector caught her just as she turned onto the road. He picked her up with one hand clasping her jaw, fingers wrapping around her neck. Pulling her nose to nose with him, he said, "If you try that again, you won't get to make this hike and see your friends."

Hector tossed her down. "Get up. Let's go." He pushed her back down the driveway and through the back yard. He marched her up the same trail he had followed with the others.

The cold wind made the hike miserable. The rain had turned to snow. "I can't wait to get back to Catalina," Hector thought. "One more day of this misery."

As they gained altitude, the snow got deeper and deeper. Hector smiled as he watched Evie struggle to walk.

"I don't think I can keep going," Evie said.

"Oh yes you can. I know about your running. You're the fittest of the bunch."

Evie stopped and he gave her a gentle push, not enough to knock her over but sufficient to let her know he meant for her to keep going. She turned and glared at him.

The wet and cold had made Hector irritable. "I almost wish she would fight," he thought. "But I don't want to expend the energy."

He answered Evie's glare with, "If you try to run, I will break a finger. If you try it a second time, I will break a wrist. You get the picture."

Evie turned and resumed the trudge up the mountain. About a mile from the shack, the snow stopped. The wind didn't. It hustled the heavy clouds away and stars began to peek through.

The temperature had plummeted. Hector's toes were freezing. He saw the snow was knee deep on Evie, and the walking just got harder. When Evie stopped, bent over and grabbed her knees, Hector didn't shove her.

"Let's rest a minute," he said. "We have a good ways to go." The cold wind penetrated his coat, and he shivered. He thought about his home on Catalina. He pictured himself sitting on the balcony looking out over the ocean.

"One more day."

Chapter 23

Sam yawned and stretched. "I think I'm going to lie down and try to sleep." He got up from the couch and stuffed the computer in the backpack he had worn on his escape attempt. Hank accompanied him to the bedroom.

"You're not getting into the bed with me, I hope," Sam said.

"No, thanks," Hank said as he walked in and checked the lock on the window one more time.

Sam was relieved when Hank stepped out and closed the door. Sam looked at his watch: 2:22am. He sat on the bed a bit and let the plan that he had hatched in the living area bang around in his mind.

"First I have to move the chest without Hank's hearing," he thought. "Socks!"

He pulled two pairs of socks from his bag and very quietly slid them under the legs of the chest they had pulled in front of the window. He turned out the light and lay down on the bed.

"I have to lie here at least thirty minutes." He checked his watch again. "What do I do after I escape? Where do I go? I will need shelter." He tried to work out his moves for when he left the house.

"I could go to our house, but that would be the first place they would look." Sam was trying to come up with where to go when he heard footsteps moving away from the door.

"It's time." Still wearing his coat, he got up, pulled on the backpack, and slid the chest away from the window. It moved easily on the socks. "We should have done that to start with," he thought.

He slowly opened the window, pushed out the screen, and crawled out. He started to walk away, then turned and closed the window.

"Now what? There is nothing to the south, so I'll head back toward town."

* * *

Arriving at the shack, Hector called out, "Wake up! You have another house guest. You know what to do by now."

Nothing happened. Hector waited an interminable minute. "Suit yourself. But it's on you if she dies right now." He aimed his gun at Evie's temple.

The door cracked open. "He has a gun aimed at her head. I think we have to toss out the shackles," James whispered. He opened the door and threw the shackles a little way.

"Not good enough. Throw farther," Hector demanded.

James pulled them back in by the cable and threw harder. They disappeared into the snow, leaving only an outline of their shape. When Hector bent down to pick them up, Evie ran. Hector tackled her before she got five steps away, nearly burying her in the deep snow.

"I'll be glad to get rid of you," he said as he dragged her by the arm back to the shackles. Dumping her face down in the snow, he put his knee on her back and attached the shackles.

Getting up, Hector said, "One more to go, then it is your big day. And I can get out of here!" He turned and tromped away back down the mountain.

"It's so much easier when the client doesn't want them to suffer a slow death," he thought.

* * *

Sam worked his way around the back of the house, through the woods, and back to the road. He noticed the rain had let up, which gave him hope for some reason.

"I wonder how long it will take them to discover I'm gone. I need to decide what to do if a car comes." Sam realized there wasn't much cover on the bay side of the road, so he crossed to the right side. "I should be able to get behind a tree over here."

He walked as quickly as he could but didn't run. He didn't know how far he had to go. He kept pushing up the road, looking back every few seconds for car lights. "I can't get caught." After a little over half an hour, Sam noticed the post office on the right, and he knew what to do next.

He crossed to the left side of the road and found the trail into Sitka National Historic Park. Relieved that he no longer had to watch over his shoulder for cars, Sam tried to focus his mind on coming up with a plan to find Evie.

He reached the bridge over Indian River and stopped to think. The sound of the river mixed with the rain. His heart hurt. "Evie is gone. My friends are gone. Dad is gone. And I'm standing here freezing and alone. God, I need some help, please," he prayed.

The rain stopped, and Sam wondered if it was an answer to his prayer. "Thanks," he said. His heart still hurt. As patches opened in the clouds, Sam could make out the water flowing beneath the bridge. The horror of having Evie snatched away fused with the ongoing grief of losing his father.

"Why is this happening, Lord? What have I done that was so bad? I feel helpless right now." Sam hung his head. "Who is doing this? Is it my own people? Harrison or Carter? What can I do?"

Sam had never felt so alone in his life. He sat down on the wet bench to think. As he tried to find direction, rage began to overtake the sorrow and self-pity. He felt the Luger in his pocket. "All I have to do is get close enough to you to fire this. But how do I find you? I could go back to the house and wait for you to find me. No, the police would come and haul me away."

As he continued to stew over the problem, his phone vibrated. He opened it. "It is time. >>>>Solar Wind," followed by GPS coordinates. He stared at the screen. "Who is this guy? Maybe he's the kidnapper. Does Solar Wind really want to help?"

His mind told him it was a bad idea to go to the location. His heart overruled. "If this leads me to the abductor, then I can kill him. If it leads me to someone who can help, that's even better."

Sam stared down at the dark water moving under the bridge. His heart seemed to sink into the river. "Why am I kidding myself? They say this guy is a trained assassin. What makes me think I can take him on? I should just go back to the house, let him get me, and get this over with."

He sighed, and as he let his breath out, he heard the flutter of wings. A large black bird landed on the rail beside him. Sam could hardly see the bird in the darkness but knew it was there.

"I guess you're looking for something to eat. Don't mind me. I'm just trying to figure out if there is any way I can save my wife. She is probably going to die."

The bird cawed loudly, and Sam jumped. "Are you a raven? I used to have a bird friend named Wingston. This guy killed him, too. I don't guess you would be interested in taking on a human project, would you?"

Sam was surprised when the bird cawed softly and hopped a step closer on the rail. "Maybe you are interested. Do you have any idea what I should do next?"

The raven hopped a few steps toward the west side of the bridge. Sam wondered if the bird was suggesting they go that way. Curious, he copied the coordinates Solar Wind had sent. He started to enter them into his GPS app and remembered that he had disabled that feature.

He stewed a minute. "Should I turn it on? If I do, the police will have a better chance of finding me. The assassin would have a better chance of finding me. If I don't, I can't follow these directions."

Finally he made his decision. He turned on the GPS feature and pasted the coordinates into the app. It directed him to go the same way the raven had flown.

"OK," Sam said. "The two of you agree, so let's go that way and see what happens." He was not surprised when the bird flew just ahead of him, leading him along rather than flying away.

Sam felt exposed with his phone traceable. He walked nervously with the bird leading the way. "I wonder if I could turn the GPS off and just follow you."

He took a few more steps and decided he needed to leave the GPS on for now. "I'm not sure about this bird yet."

Chapter 24

Sam walked into the darkness, barely able to see the raven. The winds had calmed, but it was still cold. Soft stars dotted the sky between the clouds. It was a moonless night. Something cold and wet landed on his cheek. He rubbed it off, then noticed a few snowflakes floating down.

Sam came out of the park and turned right onto Lincoln Street. He stayed vigilant, looking for headlights. The raven was still with him.

"I'm sure they know I'm gone by now. I can't let them catch me. I can't let the bad guy catch me, either," he thought. "I need a plan." Sam stewed as he walked along.

"I wish I knew where Evie is. How am I going to find her? I hope she's OK." Thinking about Evie made his heart hurt. "I can't focus on what is happening to her. I have to focus on finding her. Right now my only hope is Solar Wind. I wish I knew if he was friend or foe."

Sam continued walking and watching for car lights. With his mind grinding out ideas on what he could do, he noticed lights ahead on a side street. Adrenaline zinged his body, and he heard a caw to his left. Sam raced behind the Sitka Science Center as the car turned toward him.

Sam pressed his body behind a bush and against the building. He tensed even more as he saw the lights sweep across the parking lot. The car was turning in. He realized he was holding his breath and forced himself to breathe.

The lights went off, and Sam heard keys unlocking a door. He waited a couple of minutes then whispered to the raven, "Somebody is starting work early." He walked across the parking lot and resumed following the GPS.

"Do you really know where we are going?" Sam asked the raven. He looked at his watch. 3:52. He set a quick pace as he moved up the road. With no cars in sight and no businesses open, he relaxed, losing the fear that someone from the house would come searching for him.

The GPS app pinged a notification that he had reached his destination. "The grocery store? Really?" The store was closed and dark. "This is ridiculous!" Sam's anger surged. He felt exposed when he realized the abductor could be watching him. He hustled to the shadows on the side of the store away from the street lights and scanned the area.

His phone vibrated in his pocket. He opened it to a message. "Good. Take the Gavan Hill Trail at the end of Baranof Street. Two miles in, take the side trail to the left. >>>>Solar Wind," followed by more coordinates. "I hope this isn't a wild goose chase," Sam said. As he was copying the coordinates, the raven cawed. He looked up to see car lights illuminating the road, coming from the opposite side of the building.

Sam pushed his body against the building. At the last minute, he remembered to pull the gun out of his pocket. He held his breath and watched as a state patrol car drove slowly by. He breathed again as the taillights moved out of sight.

He remembered his encounter with Dirk Donegan when he had failed to release the safety. He stepped back into the light, located the safety, and released it. "I need to be ready."

Sam scanned the area again, seeing no one. He began walking toward the trailhead. He was so cold. "If Solar Wind is the abductor, he could be anywhere." After another quarter of a mile another thought came. "Or he could be leading me to where he is holding Evie." His energy surged and he pushed on.

Passing a convenience store, Sam realized how hungry he was. The store had just opened, so he turned in and bought a dozen energy bars, five bottles of water, and a mocha coffee. He paid with his bank card, stuffed the waters and all but two of the energy bars into his back pack, and opened a bar and the coffee.

The raven cawed at him when he came out. "I needed something to eat and drink," Sam explained. The raven cawed again and flew ahead as if urging him on. Sam ate and drank as he walked.

He finished the coffee and two energy bars just as he got to the trailhead. "How convenient." There was a trash can just ahead. "I should probably stop and think about the sanity of walking into the wilderness based on an anonymous message and having no idea where Evie is," he thought as he tossed his cup and wrappers into the can.

* * *

Hector set his alarm, slid into bed, and pulled the covers up. "I shouldn't have to work again after this job," he thought as he settled down for a nap. "One more to go. I'm betting they will try to move him. I hope it's not too far away. This last one will be the hardest. I doubt I'll have the help of a storm, either. I'll come up with a plan after I rest."

Hector was good at resting when he needed to. He pictured sitting on the balcony of his home on Catalina and imagined the breeze blowing gently and the sound of the waves rising up from the ocean. In minutes he was asleep.

* * *

Fear, longing, and rage urged Sam on as he started down the trail. "I just have to get her back. How could I have let him get her? I never should have left the bedroom. If only I had stayed with her."

A wave of guilt rolled through his soul, mixing with the other strong emotions. Sam realized he was stomping the ground as he walked and going so fast he was giving out of breath. "I need to slow down and stop making so much noise. If the killer is out here, I am making myself too easy a target."

Sam stopped dead in his tracks when he realized he had used the word killer. "I can't think like that. I have to stay positive. I am going to rescue Evie. I am going to rescue all of them. There will be no killing. I just can't let that happen."

He took a deep breath and resumed walking without the stomping. "I wish I had a plan. Maybe I can think of one as I go." He stewed as he walked. "It's hard to plan when I don't even know where I'm going or whom I will find when I get there. My best option is to stay alert and keep my hand on this gun." He gripped the handle of the gun in his coat pocket and kept walking.

About a mile in, the trail started to climb steeply. Within a couple of minutes, Sam stepped into the first patch of snow. The higher he climbed, the deeper the snow got. It was nearly knee deep when Sam stopped and thought. "How am I going to find a side trail in this?"

With snow all around him, the world didn't seem so dark. He could see the raven on a branch just ahead. "I don't suppose you know where this trail is?" Sam asked. The raven flared his wings then tucked them back in.

"Wow! I didn't realize how big you are," Sam said. Suddenly it dawned on him that he needed to keep quiet. He looked around quickly but saw no one.

* * *

Joe had fallen asleep on the couch. Hank was feeling sleepy too. "I need more coffee," he thought and headed to the kitchen.

Wendy, who had come in at Joe's request after Bill was sent to the emergency room, looked up from her phone. "All's quiet so far," she said.

"I can't believe that guy got in with two of us on guard," Hank said. "He has some serious skills. Don't take any chances."

"I'm staying right here until someone walks through that door. Then he'll have this to deal with," she said patting her service weapon. "I'll shoot and ask questions later. The door is locked, so no one but the perpetrator is likely to come in."

"Sounds like a good plan," Hank answered. He poured a cup of coffee.

"Do you think there is any chance they are still alive? How many has this guy taken?" Wendy asked.

"Bryant thinks he is gathering them up for a mass killing and will make Sam watch."

"That's horrible."

"Yeah. But as long as we can keep Sam out of his hands, there is a chance we can find them."

"Let's make sure Sam stays safe, then."

"I think I'll poke my head into his room just to make sure."

Hank quietly opened the door and looked into the darkness. He couldn't really see, so he opened it a little farther. He spilled some of his coffee when he saw the bed empty and the chest away from the window.

"Joe!" Hank yelled.

Joe came flying down the hall.

"Sam's gone," Hank said as he pulled back the curtain.

"Oh no!" Joe said. "I didn't expect another attack until tomorrow since he has been taking one a day."

"The window is unlocked, and I don't see any signs of forced entry."

"Look," Joe said pointing to the socks under the chest legs. "I think Sam took off on his own."

"Man! I should have expected something like that. How could he be that stupid!"

"Stupid is right," Joe said. "Now we have to devote resources to searching for him as well as looking for the other victims." He pulled out his phone and called Bryant.

"I hate to wake you, but we have had a bad night. The perpetrator broke in during the storm, chloroformed Bill and took

Evie. Now it looks like Sam went out through a window to try to find her."

"It has been a bad night," Bryant answered. "Sam may have just cost six people their lives."

Chapter 25

Sam trudged through the knee-deep snow feeling cold and stressed. "This is ridiculous. I'm never going to find her. He is probably going to shoot me before I ever see him."

The impossibility of the situation weighed on Sam, but something kept him moving forward. "I have to find her. There is no giving up, and this is the best plan I have." Yearning for his precious wife, Sam kept walking.

Trees were all around him, and undergrowth blocked his path. Sam looked around. "I'm off the trail." The snow was so deep he couldn't see where the path was. "I think I should be going uphill." So that's the way he walked, hoping he wasn't lost.

* * *

"Have you alerted the State Patrol?" Bryant asked.

"That's my next call," Joe answered.

"After you do that, get everyone at the house together and make a list of places Sam is likely to have gone. Send Hank to their house immediately."

"I hope he didn't get another message from Solar Wind. If he did, there is no telling where he might be heading."

"Umm," Bryant said. "I'll be right over."

After alerting the State Patrol dispatcher, Joe called everyone to the living area. Sleepy people converged in the living area.

"It appears Sam sneaked out the window and took off. We need to find him before the perpetrator does. Please try to think of anywhere Sam might be going. We need to figure out his next move so we can intercept him before he does something stupid. Well, something even more stupid than going off on his own."

"He will try to find Evie," Skauty said. "I feel like that is stating the obvious. Since we have found no signs of the abductor in town, I suspect he is in the wilderness. We should start searching trails."

"There are a lot of trails around here," Joe said. "What makes you think Sam would venture out of town?"

"He's smart. He will figure that out," Skauty said.

Joe read the certainty on Skauty's face. He didn't want to admit it, but knew he was right. "That's where we should have been looking all along," he thought to himself with regret.

Joe called the State Patrol dispatcher back. "We need to get units to as many trailheads as possible. I think that's where our escapee may be headed."

* * *

Dodging trees and undergrowth made the walking slow. Sam forced himself not to panic. "I can do this." He heard an insistent caw to his left.

"I almost forgot about you," Sam said. He trusted the raven was trying to lead him back to the trail and went toward the bird. When he got back to the raven, he could tell there was a divide in the trees. "That must be the trail. Thanks."

Sam kept trudging, trying to stay in what looked like a trail. The virgin snow made it difficult to tell. He had walked forever it seemed, bound in the snow and mountains. Pulling out his phone, he studied the GPS app. "That's got to be more than two miles. How am I ever going to find a side trail? I can hardly stay on the main trail."

The raven cawed and flew about thirty feet off the left of the trail. Sam looked carefully. "That is not a trail," he said to the bird.

Sam looked at the app again. The destination appeared to be slightly northeast of where he was standing. The raven cawed again.

"Alright. Alright. I'll follow you."

Sam continued to gain elevation as he followed the raven's zigzag course through the trees. The snow got deeper, reaching all the way to his knees. The walking got harder and harder.

Sam kept an eye on the app, and the pin got closer. Watching the phone, he tripped over a fallen log. He let go of the phone as he went down, catching himself on his hands. Getting back up and brushing the snow off, his breath caught in his throat when he realized the phone was gone.

He stood still and scanned the area around where his hands had made holes in the snow. "That was stupid. I can't afford stupid mistakes."

While he chastised himself, he heard a vibrating sound to his right. He noticed a rectangular indentation in the snow and found his phone about three inches down. Skauty was calling.

Isolated in the snowy wilderness, Sam longed to hear the familiar voice. He suspected they would try to track him if he answered. He declined the call and let it go to voicemail.

"I have to get back on track. I have to find this guy and stop him. I just wish I knew where he was and how I am going to do that." He studied his phone and looked at the raven. "I think it's time to turn the GPS off and trust the raven."

Resuming his march into nowhere, Sam tried to watch the ground as well as the bird. Faint light began to do battle with the night sky in the east. The light brought renewed hope to Sam's heart.

He pushed on until he worried he had gone too far. The raven kept leading him on. Wariness crept in, and Sam grasped the handle of the gun as he looked around. "Trees. Trees and snow. But what was that?"

In the distance there was something dark against the snow that was too short to be a tree.

"It could definitely be a man. Maybe in a hood." He slid the gun out of his pocket and approached.

* * *

Hector rose with the first inkling of dawn. Shaking off sleep and fatigue, he made coffee and grabbed three energy bars. He checked his phone and saw that Joe's car was on the move. Relieved that they hadn't found the tracking device, Hector watched the dot move on the screen.

"Where are you going? Do you have my target with you?" He chewed a bite and sipped coffee. "I hope you're not going home to sleep. I know you had a restless night."

He followed the movement of the vehicle. It stopped at the Gavan Hill Trailhead. After three minutes, it moved on. "Interesting." The car moved up and down the streets, going slowly. "Odd."

The car stopped again. Hector wrote down the trailhead and the address of the second stop. "A bed and breakfast. Could be." The next stop was another bed and breakfast. Then a motel.

"You have discovered the tracking device and are trying to give me so many locations I can't cover them all." Hector opened his second energy bar and pondered. "If you found the device, then Sam is probably not with you at all. Someone else would be moving him."

He looked at his empty coffee mug and poured more. "Maybe you are surveying possible locations to stash him. But why stop at a trailhead? Why would you be running all over the place?"

* * *

When Joe got the call that State Patrol officers had driven around the various trailheads and found nothing, he slammed his hand on the counter, rattling the coffee maker. "Where could the idiot be?"

"He has had time to get out of town by now," Skauty said coming up behind him.

Joe jumped. "Sorry, I'm a little tense."

"That's understandable."

"If he has gone out into the wilderness, we'll never find him. It would be the proverbial needle in a haystack, and I only have a few officers."

"We could organize search parties to go out. That would increase our reach."

"I'm afraid that would be too dangerous. If anyone encounters the perpetrator, it would be a blood bath."

"I see he cut down a tree as a diversion," Bryant said as he arrived at the kitchen."

"Hey, Bryant. We have a major mess," Joe responded.

"You and Hank have had a rough night. Go home and rest. I'll take it from here."

"Like that's going to happen! There is no way I could sleep right now. I think we need to check the motels and B and Bs to see if Sam checked in. Do you think satellite images could show a new building off the grid?"

"I'll get the office working on that right now," Bryant said.

"Gary and Jordan should be here soon. I'm going to start with motels and B and Bs in the north."

"OK. I'll send one of the others to check in the south."

"Stay alert. The perpetrator may be back."

Joe backed his car out of the garage and drove north. His first stop was the Gavan Hill trailhead. He looked down the trail. "I wonder if you went that way."

Chapter 26

As Sam drew close enough to make out details, black stringy hair, a scraggly black beard, and black coat came into focus. "Revenge is devils' work. And the devils are working."

"Jolly?" Sam said stupefied.

"Jolly? It will do."

"What have you done with Evie?" Sam demanded, aiming the gun at Jolly's chest.

"Nothing."

"Where is she?"

"No need for the gun. Come to the house. Let's talk."

"I'm not going anywhere until I get answers."

Jolly turned and started walking away. "Shoot me if you like. It won't matter. I died a long time ago. If you kill me, you will never find them. If you just stand there, you will never find them. Bring the bird, too."

Sam's feet were frozen from both cold and indecision. The gun was now aimed at Jolly's back, and Jolly was getting farther away. "Should I shoot? Should I follow? Should I go back and start over?"

The raven flew in Jolly's direction and cawed softly. That was the nudge Sam needed, and he followed, keeping the gun at the ready.

Sam followed Jolly about a quarter of a mile before he saw a structure. "House? Building? What is this?" Sam wondered.

Rising in the snow was a structure roofed with solar panels that were white, mimicking the snow. But they had no snow on them.

Sam saw five huge satellite dishes pointing in various directions. They all looked like snow but, like the solar panels, had no snow on them. Sam stood gawking and didn't realize he had stopped walking.

"What in the world?" Hearing the door close brought Sam back. "OK, do I go in? Is this Solar Wind? What am I getting into?" He stood trying to sort the conflicting thoughts and feelings. He wasn't sure how long he had stood there when he heard the raven caw from the roof.

"I have come this far. I guess I might as well see what this is about." He stepped through the door into a room lit by computer monitors. They covered the wall. He counted five consoles with keyboards and joysticks, one rolling office chair, and a dog bed.

As Sam took in the scene, he realized all the monitors had images of various nature scenes, hiding their true content. He recovered from his amazement and walked into the next room. It was a kitchen with a bed. Another door led outside.

Sam cringed when it dawned on him that Jolly was not there. "Where are you?" he called. No answer. He went back into the front room and looked closely. Jolly wasn't there. He jumped when the back door opened, aiming his gun in that direction.

Jolly came in with a bucket of water, followed by a beautiful husky. The dog caught Sam's scent and bristled and growled. It charged and backed Sam against the wall.

"Calm. Place," Jolly commanded. The dog growled one more time and went to the bed.

"We don't have visitors." The dog continued to snarl. "This is Thor. He needed water," he said as he poured some into a bowl. "Up."

Thor walked to the bowl, eyeing Sam and snarling. "I'd put the gun away. But suit yourself."

Sam put the gun into his coat pocket, and Thor stopped snarling. Sam was so addled from the dog's charging him that he stood there speechless.

"Food?"

"No, thanks," Sam said.

"Coffee?"

Being so cold and weary, Sam couldn't resist. "Thanks." Sam's nerves tightened when Jolly poured two cups from a pot that was already brewed. "You knew I was coming."

"Yes."

"You're Solar Wind," Sam stated as he made the connection.

"Yes."

"You live here by yourself?"

"No. Thor."

"Where is Evie?"

"I can't tell you that."

"But you said you would help me find her."

"No. I said we could stop these monsters."

"Do you know where she is?"

"Yes."

Sam pulled the gun. Before he could aim, Thor landed on his chest, knocking him to the floor and grabbing his wrist in his mouth.

"I'd drop the gun."

Sam let go of the pistol, and Thor let go of his wrist.

"He doesn't like guns."

* * *

Joe stopped at the bed and breakfast and knocked. He kept knocking till he finally woke the proprietor, who was in her robe when she answered the door.

"Joe Ford, Chief of Police," he flashed his badge. Holding up a picture of Sam, he asked, "Did this man check in last night."

"No, I haven't seen him."

"He is in danger. If you see him, please call me," Joe said, giving her his card.

After covering three bed and breakfasts and two motels, Joe decided that Skauty was right. "He went into the wilderness."

Joe called Bryant, "I haven't found anything. I think Skauty was right. Sam went out of the city. It was dumb of me to think he checked into a B and B. I have wasted time. Any luck with the satellite images?"

"Not yet. They are still looking, though."

"I'm heading back. Do you think we need to move the rest of the folks?"

"I don't see that it would do any good. This guy seems to be able to find us wherever we are."

"I wonder how he does that?" Joe mused. "I'll see you in a bit."

Joe stomped into the house. "Look what I found!" he said, holding up the tracking device. "It was on my car."

"That explains a lot. I think we have two options. We can move the people and leave the tracking device here. Or we can move the tracking device and leave the people here. Since this is so comfortable, I'd opt for the latter. Let's find a vacant building and stash the device there. If he storms it, no one will get hurt."

"I'll get Jordan on that. I'm going to try to sleep a couple of hours. I'll use Sam and Evie's room."

"We'll have to park your car at the building to make it believable," Bryant pointed out.

"OK, I'll get out anything I need."

* * *

Hector studied Joe's movements all the way back to the house. His mind kept being pulled back to the trailhead. "But why go to a bunch of different locations? You either found the tracking device or think I'm following you."

He pulled up a map of the trail. "I see. Shelters. Get him out of town and maybe I can't find him. I think it's time to go for a hike."

Hector pocketed his taser, packed several energy bars and water into his backpack, and opened his gun case. He looked at them with disdain. "I don't like guns. They are too loud. I much prefer a knife or my bare hands, but I may need you."

He holstered a handgun and pulled out a Winchester and 30/06 cartridges. "I'll meet you at the shelter."

* * *

Thor backed away from Sam, and Sam got up. Keeping an eye on the dog, he tentatively picked up the gun and put it back into his pocket. Thor seemed satisfied and lay down on his bed.

"Why won't you tell me where they are?" Sam asked.

"Because I need you to take down the devils."

"What do you mean?"

"They think they are getting revenge on you. But we can turn the tables. We can get revenge on the devils. We can bring down the entire system and establish a new order."

"What system?"

"The feudal system that the A-30 has created."

"You're absolutely crazy!"

"We will leverage these killings to convince Congress to dismantle the power the A-30 has amassed."

Chapter 27

Sam went numb. His vision blurred and became tunnel-like. Jolly pulled up the chair and pushed him into it. It finally registered that Jolly was speaking.

"Put your head between your knees," he was saying. Sam complied, and the blurry fog began to clear. The only thing he could remember that Jolly had said was "killings."

"You said killings. Do you mean they are already dead?"

"No, but they will be."

Sam popped up from the chair, anger surging. "If they aren't dead, there is still time to save them. I need to know where they are!"

Thor growled but stayed in his bed.

"Hector has never failed a mission, and his mandate is to cause all of you to suffer a slow death."

"Hector?"

"Hector Hoffman is a world class assassin. He has been used by several governments and numerous folks who are wealthy enough to hire him. To date, he has never failed a mission."

"I have to try to save them!" Sam yelled, and Thor stood. "You have to tell me where they are."

Jolly glanced at Thor, and the dog seemed to calm.

"I'm sorry, but it will do no good for you to know where they are. We need to get to work telling the president and Congress about what is happening."

Sam couldn't believe what he was hearing. "This guy really is insane," he thought.

"I can tell that you find this situation incredible. As you have seen, I am adept at hacking into systems and controlling information. I know, for example, that you disabled the GPS function on your phone once you got close. That is good because Hector won't be able to trace you."

"How can you know that?"

Jolly walked into the front room and sat down at one of the keyboards. He opened a program and told Sam to look. Sam was amazed to see his phone's settings on the screen.

"How can you do that?"

"I have skills. And a lot of computer power."

"I don't care about your skills or your computers. What I care about is saving my wife and friends. And you're going to help me do that!" Sam reached into his pocket, and Thor was beside him with his hackles up.

"If I tell you where they are, you will die, too," Jolly said calmly. "And they will have succeeded. If I keep you alive, we have a chance to break this terrible system and restore hope to a whole country."

"You are insane! There is no way you can do that."

"I have already started."

"What?"

"I have been feeding the president and certain members of Congress emails about the A-30's activities. When we let them know about this latest atrocity, they will want you to come testify."

Again, Sam couldn't believe what he was hearing. He wanted to believe Jolly was insane, but his heart was telling him otherwise. He pulled into himself, trying to figure out what to do. Finally, he realized Jolly was talking.

"You are the one who knows about the nuclear waste dumping. You are the one who knows they blew up a shipment of radioactive material. You are the one who knows about the fish thing and the attempt to resettle an entire town by force. And you are the one that knows about these kidnappings and murders."

"Who exactly is behind this?"

"Mitch Carter and Holmes Harrison went together on the contract with Hector."

"So it's not a Tlingit thing."

"No. There were some people unhappy about your becoming chief, but they wouldn't do anything like this. Your people value life."

Sam's mind raced trying to figure out what to do. He decided to fish for information.

"How do you know it is Carter and Harrison behind this?"

"I intercept phone signals."

"How does Hector plan to kill them?"

"I don't know exactly. They wanted all of you to suffer and for you to have to watch the others die."

"If he doesn't have me, will he kill the others?"

"Probably, but I can't know for sure. He doesn't know where you are, so I think we are safe."

"How do you know where the others are?"

"I can track him like I track you."

"How did you know I was up that night Hector tried to break in?"

"By the movement of your phone."

"Can you show me where Hector is right now?"

"No."

"Why not?"

"I don't think that is wise. I need to keep you away from him."

"Do you honestly think I am just going to sit here and wait while he kills my wife?"

"I hope so. I know it's hard to lose her and your friends. But think of how many millions of people you can help. The nation is in terrible shape. So many people are dying of starvation that we can't even count them. You are their only hope."

A heavy weight crashed onto Sam's heart. What Jolly said made unsettling sense. The people he saw in Buena Vista flashed into his mind. He remembered how hungry they had looked and how grateful they were for the little bit of food they had shared. He thought about how James's family had died of hunger.

The weight seemed so heavy that Sam sank to the floor. He knew the evil of which two of the A-30 members were capable. "I suppose the others are just as bad," he thought. "How can I make a choice like this? It is too hard."

"This is war. It's a war for the survival of our country," Jolly continued. "In war you expect casualties. It is inevitable that some will die. That doesn't stop a country from waging war to protect itself."

"No! There has to be another way!" Sam nearly yelled.

"I wish there were another way. I really do. But I can't think of one. The moment has finally come to break the devils' grasp. You and I can do this. We will take the country back and let it return to being a nation of liberty and justice for all."

Sam wanted to run out of the house and keep running until he found Evie. He stood. "I have to find her," he said and hurried out the door. But he had no idea where to go. That thought slowed his steps.

"If you leave you will all die for nothing. Evie and the others are going to die anyway. You can at least make their deaths mean something," Jolly called from the front door.

Sam was stopped by the conflict in his soul. He couldn't keep going. He couldn't turn back. He couldn't just stand there, either. Time was passing. Evie's life depended on him. He had to do something. A thought finally came that seemed plausible. "I will have to get on Jolly's computers and find her. That's my best chance. I can't live if I just let her die for this psycho's scheme."

Sam turned and walked back to the house, determined to act as though he was cooperating and to see if he could get Jolly to let his guard down. Another thought quickened his steps.

"Why don't you send the police to where he is holding the others while we inform Congress?"

"I'm afraid that won't work. It takes a lot of death and tragedy to get Congress to move on anything. They won't easily betray the people who funded their elections."

Sam's heart sank again. His head drooped as he walked back through the door. "How am I going to get to her? I wish I never had come here," he thought. Then he said it: "I should never have come here."

"You made the right choice for so many people. You will save a nation and be a hero."

"I don't feel like a hero. I feel like the sorriest scumbag on the planet."

"If it's any help, I lost my family to starvation because of the A-30."

"What do you mean?"

"I had a wife and two kids. They all got sick and died. That's when I moved to Alaska and decided to bring down this terrible system."

"I'm sorry," Sam said. He looked Jolly in the eye and wasn't sure he believed him. "He said it so flatly," he thought. A surge of fear ran through. "What if this is all a lie, and he is holding me till Hector gets here? What if the others are nearby? What if he is Hector?"

Chapter 28

"Now that's interesting," Hector said to himself as he checked the police chief's location once more before leaving. The car was at a factory building.

Hector did a quick search on the building. "It's been closed for seven years. Were the earlier movements a decoy? He is creating quite the puzzle. I wonder if he found the tracking device. It doesn't matter."

He pondered his next move. "This changes things. I think I will check out the building before hiking to the shelter. It fits with what they have done so far. It also makes more sense than a bed and breakfast."

Hector stroked his chin as he thought. "I need to shave," he said, distracted by the stubble. He zoomed in on the factory and studied the surrounding area. "I need another vehicle, but I don't have time for that."

He opened the garage. The Jeep Gladiator was in the back. It's front end was largely spared in the crash because of the winch. "I'm sure they know the Hummer. They may or may not have seen the Jeep. I'll take the Jeep. It's easier to get out anyway. I'll need this little guy, too," he said to himself as he grabbed a second backpack containing a wall penetrating radar device.

He laid the backpacks and the rifle in the bed and drove about a quarter of a mile past the factory. He found a place to pull off the road into the woods and parked there. He changed his mind and placed the rifle inside with the other backpack. With his handgun, knife, and backpack, he set off.

Hector worked his way through the woods to the back of the building. He could see Joe's patrol car parked near the side door. He set up the wall penetrating radar device on a tripod.

"There are two bodies in there. It's worth finding out if one is Sam." He returned the radar device to the backpack and sneaked up to the back door. Very gently, he tried the door. "Locked. Hmm, do I pick it or just knock?"

* * *

Joe gave up after thirty minutes of attempted napping. It wasn't happening. He went back to the den.

"I thought you were going to nap," Bryant said.

"I couldn't sleep. Do you need me to drive my car to the building?"

"No, I already sent two officers. If he falls for it, we should apprehend him."

"I just hope no one gets shot." He pulled out the map of the area and studied it. "The closest trail to here is Mount Verstovia. I wonder if that's where Sam went."

Bryant looked over the map. "Maybe. But if he got a message from that Solar Wind person, there is no telling where he went. I don't guess you have any idea who this Solar Wind could be."

"Not a clue. My best guess would be the perpetrator."

"I guess that's possible, but my gut is telling me otherwise."

"I think I agree. We need to start checking out trails."

"I don't think we have the people to go on wild goose chases in the woods. Whom would you send?"

"You're right. I'll have to go. Mount Verstovia is only a couple of miles. It won't take me long."

"I don't think it's wise for you to go out alone."

"I don't think we have another option."

* * *

Hector chuckled at the thought of knocking on the door and what the guard's expression would be then knelt down to pick the lock. The door creaked on its hinges, so he left it open. He crept quietly to the end of the hall and listened. Music was coming from the right, the direction he expected the people to be. He readied his pistol and moved in that direction.

He came to an office with windows half the height of the wall. The music seemed to be coming from there. When he leaned to peek in, he saw two officers at a table, playing cards.

Hector pulled back, frustrated. "A decoy. Stupid. Stupid. Stupid. They found the tracker. Wasted time."

He stood thinking. "I could storm the room and force them to tell me where he is. I could assume he is at one of the shelters on that trail. If he's not there, I will have wasted more time. I need answers. I have a time line. This has to be done by five o'clock."

Hector crouched below the window and moved to the door. He tested it as quietly as he could. "Locked."

The music was loud enough to cover the noise Hector made as he picked the lock. He grinned at the plan that formed in his mind. Quietly and slowly, he pulled the door open and crouched behind it.

"What in the world! Who's there?" he heard one officer say. Chairs slid, and he readied himself. When the first officer stepped through the door, Hector launched, grabbing him in a choke hold and aiming his pistol at the second officer.

"Drop your weapon," Hector ordered. When the officer in the choke hold went limp, he lowered him to the floor and picked up his gun.

"Have a seat," he said, picking up the second gun and directing the remaining officer to the table. "Thank you, I believe I will," he said as he pulled a doughnut from the box.

"What do you want?" the officer asked.

"You probably know what, since you are stationed here."

"You're the assassin," the officer said.

Hector cringed. He didn't like to be called an assassin. It sounded so evil.

"I have killed no one yet. I hope you're not going to be the first." The officer was young and fit, so Hector kept his gun aimed at him and stayed vigilant. His name tag said Joseph Helman.

"Joseph, I need you to tell me where Sam Hanson is. If you cooperate, neither you nor your partner will be hurt."

The other officer started to stir, coming to. Hector dragged him into the room, then resumed talking to Joseph. "I'm waiting."

Joseph sat silently. Hector turned the gun to the officer on the ground. "The first shot will be a knee. You have five seconds. Four. Three."

"I don't know where he is."

"Two."

"He ran off, and we haven't been able to find him."

"One."

"That's the truth!" The pleading in Joseph's voice convinced Hector he was telling the truth.

"Why are you here with the police chief's car?"

"They found the tracking device and wanted to lure you here. They thought we could catch you if you showed up."

Hector smiled. They obviously didn't know with whom they were dealing. "Where do you suspect Hanson went?"

"I have no idea. We've been searching the town but haven't located him."

Hector was conflicted with possibilities as thoughts crashed in his head. "Maybe he is lying to cover up where they hid him. If he is telling the truth and Sam ran off, he could be anywhere." He decided to try one more time.

At that moment, the other officer stood up. He looked dazed, so Hector grabbed him and stuffed him into the other chair. "I think you're lying," he said to Joseph and aimed the gun at the other officer's knee.

"I swear it's the truth. They said Hanson sneaked out of the house last night and they haven't found him. Chief Ford apparently wondered how you found the house until he discovered the tracking device."

Hector was pleased with the fear he saw in Joseph's eyes. "I think he's telling the truth," he thought. The now-conscious officer reached for his radio. Like lightning, Hector grabbed his hand and twisted his arm back. The metal conference table had open rails underneath. Holstering his gun, Hector handcuffed him to the table through one of the openings.

"You're next," Hector said. "Give me your cuffs." He handcuffed Joseph to the table, pulled out his knife, and cut the wires of their radios.

As Hector walked out of the building, he could hear banging as the officers wrestled with the table. He took time to let the air out of two tires on the patrol car then headed back to the Jeep.

His mind raced with possibilities of what to do next. "I have to find Sam and have him at the shack by five." The pressure was mounting. "It's so much easier when I can kill and be done with it. I don't think I'll ever take a job like this again." Then he smiled. "Actually, I won't ever have to work again."

Hector sat in the Jeep trying to decide his next move. "It makes sense that if the State Patrol can't find Sam in town, then maybe he's not in town." He pulled up a map centered at the house from which he had abducted Evie. There were four potential trails leading out of town. "I need to rethink this. He will be hunting his wife, not hiding. Where would I look for me? Hmmm."

Hector thought about the situation. "But he's not looking for me. He's looking for his wife. The police haven't been able to find my targets. If I were Sam and I were smart, I'd look where they haven't. Would he assume the same thing I initially thought? Yes, that's what he would do."

Hector pulled up maps of the four trails he had found, looking for shelters. His phone vibrated.

"Hanson not at factory. Decoy," the text said.

"You're a little late for that," Hector said out loud.

"The Gavan Hill Trail has a shelter. But what will he do when he finds no one is there? What would I do? I'd come back and try another trail."

Hector checked his watch. "Seven twenty-five. I should be able to catch him on his way back. Now how do I get there?"

He studied his map. "It looks like the quickest access is from the end of Pherson street." He entered the trailhead into his GPS and took off.

Parking at the trailhead, Hector said to himself, "I was beginning to worry, but now I think I'll be able to finish the job early. Sam Hanson, I'm coming for you."

Chapter 29

Sam stood paralyzed in the front room of Jolly's little house. He tried to sort out the thoughts flying through his mind and the feelings flooding his heart.

He started with his last thought, "Could this be Hector?" He decided that was unlikely. "If he were Hector, he would already have tied me up or something. I think I have to believe what he says. But I can't let Evie die. I just can't. I have to play along with him until I can find out where she is, no matter what it costs the nation."

A surge of rage filled Sam's heart, but he squelched it and said, "So what do we do now?"

"We wait."

"We wait? What do you mean, we wait?" Sam's stomach did a flip.

"We wait until it is done, then we notify the authorities, Congress, and the president."

Sam's knees weakened, and his vision blurred. Jolly seemed to be saying something, but Sam couldn't hear. Visions of Evie being tortured to death floated through his mind.

A hand was on his shoulder, easing him into a chair. The hand pushed his head between his knees, and his mind began to clear. He thought he was going to retch, but that seemed to clear, too.

"You need something to eat," Sam heard through the fog. "This is going to be a hard day."

Sam lifted his head and tried to remember when he had eaten last. It seemed so far away, but it was really the energy bars last night. A wave of fatigue washed over as he watched Jolly walk to the kitchen.

He hated Jolly in that moment, hated his greasy black hair, hated his bushy beard, and hated the fact that he was right. "I do need to eat."

Sam heard a pan hit the stove. "I'll have some eggs ready in a bit," Jolly called out.

"Thanks," Sam managed. Then it dawned on him that he was alone with Jolly's computers. He spun around in the chair and wiggled the mouse of the computer on which Jolly had shown him his phone. He was surprised it opened without a password. "He is usually the only one here, though," he thought.

He minimized the program and began looking for something that would lead him to Evie. He felt a presence before he heard, "You won't find her. She's not on that computer," Jolly said. "How do you want your eggs?"

"It doesn't matter," Sam fumed. "Do you mind if I check my email?"

"Help yourself. The eggs will be scrambled soon, though."

Instead of email, Sam logged onto the program used for tracking cell phones. He searched for Evie's but found nothing. Then he remembered it was off. He tried to remember David's number. The first one he entered was in Iowa. He tried again, and the program showed the phone was at David's house.

"I have no idea what Viviana's number is," he thought.

"Having any luck?" Jolly asked, and Sam jumped. "Keep in mind that Hector knows what he is doing. He wouldn't make the mistake of letting himself be tracked by a cell phone. Here are your eggs."

Sam took the plate and set the cup of coffee on the desk by the keyboard he had been using. He noticed a nervous expression come over Jolly. Jolly was staring at the cup.

"What?" Sam asked.

"I usually set drinks on the floor so that if they spill no electronics will be damaged."

Sam gingerly set the cup on the floor. "Better?"

"Thanks."

With his first bite of eggs, Sam realized how hungry he was. He devoured the rest.

Jolly sat on the floor with a plate of eggs just as Sam was finishing his. Thor walked over and sniffed. Jolly fed him a bite with his fork. That seemed to satisfy Thor, and he went back to his bed.

Sam watched the interaction and wondered what it must be like to live alone with just a dog. Jolly ate silently, not looking up. Sam thought he had forgotten he was there and slowly turned back to the computer.

"You won't find them."

Sam looked back. Jolly was still eating.

"And if you do, you can't save them. You have to accept that. You can save yourself but not them." Jolly started rocking and humming. Thor came over and licked him on the face. Jolly didn't stop.

Sam thought, "Maybe this guy is insane." He spun around and tried to open the computer's list of programs. It required biometric scans to open anything beyond the internet, which Sam had used to open his tracking program.

Jolly still hummed and rocked. Sam couldn't make out the song. Like turning off a light, Jolly stopped, finished his eggs, picked up Sam's plate, and went to the kitchen.

Sam quickly looked for alternate ways to open the computer, like a password. "Nothing," he said to himself. "What am I going to do?" Sam's chest tightened with panic. He heard dishes clanging in the kitchen as Jolly washed them. Finally an idea formed.

"Don't you want to know where Hector is?" Sam called out.

"No."

"If I am his ultimate victim and his is as talented as you say, he won't give up until he finds me."

"He is searching in Sitka. The police chief went to a bunch of locations looking for you. That should keep Hector busy."

"When was the last time you checked?"

"Just before you arrived."

"How do you track him if his GPS is off?"

Jolly didn't respond.

"He may figure out I'm not in the city and come this way."

"I can't imagine why."

* * *

Hector set off up the trail. "I hope this isn't a wild goose chase, but I can't think of a more likely option. If he's not at the shelter, what will I do? I need to think of my next step as I walk. I'll have to concentrate. At least the scenery is pretty.

When he had gained enough elevation, he came to the snow. At first he wasn't one hundred percent sure. But as the snow deepened, he looked up the trail and smiled. "This is better than I had hoped." A single set of footprints marred the pristine snow. "You really are alone."

Hector pulled up the map of the trail and studied the terrain between the shelter and the shack where he held the others. "It's a lot shorter to cut across the mountains, but there is no trail. I think I'll have time to come back this way. Then again, there is zero chance of running into interference if I cut across. I'll ponder that as I walk."

He took a few steps then stopped again. Opening his phone he studied the area around the shelter. "About here I need to loop around and approach from the back. Payday is getting close."

Hector hastened his pace. He could almost smell his prey.

* * *

The irritating humming started again. Sam walked into the kitchen, and Jolly was standing at the sink, rocking back and forth. He seemed in a trance.

"Yes," Jolly said and went to one of the computers. When he put his ring finger on the scanner, the computer opened to a screen with Hector's location.

"Oh. He's coming," Jolly whispered. "Did you activate the GPS on your phone?" he yelled.

"No."

"You have to hide. Get your coat and go behind the outhouse. If you hear the door open, run."

"How close is he?"

"He's where I met you when you turned off the trail. Go. Go. Go!" he urged as he pushed Sam's coat into his hands. The last thing Sam heard as he went out the back door was, "Thor, ready."

Chapter 30

Sam didn't go behind the outhouse. He stopped at the back corner of Jolly's house and peeked around. Not seeing the tracks they had made coming to the house, he moved to the front corner. He pulled the gun from his coat pocket. He was breathing hard with an adrenaline rush.

He heard snow crunching under Jolly's feet, then a realization hit. "What if he left the computer open?" He sneaked toward the back door, carefully stepping in his previous footprints to minimize the sound. He slipped through the door. Thor eyed him as he approached the computer.

Sam could see Jolly waiting about a hundred feet from the house. Another surge of adrenaline hit when he saw the screen still showing Hector's location. Without sitting down, he started clicking to see if he could find a history of locations.

He realized he was sweating, nerves tense and zinging. In his hurry, he clicked the wrong spot with the mouse and the program disappeared. He cringed till he realized he had just minimized it. He brought it back up and continued hunting. He looked out the window to make sure Jolly wasn't coming. He could see Hector in the distance. Approaching.

"I have to find them." He went back to the computer.

"Yes!" he said to himself when a map popped up showing the last twenty-four hours. He found how to expand the history to the last week. Studying the map, he located his house. Then he noticed a house just down the street from him that was a daily location.

From there, his eyes were drawn to a place on the side of a mountain. He had gone there five times. Sam counted, "Evie, David, Viviana, James, Sandy. Five. The last time he was there was in the middle of the night, about three hours after Evie was taken. That has to be it!"

He took a picture of the screen, then was able to pull up the coordinates for the location. As he captured a picture of that screen, he heard Jolly talking.

"Hello! I don't get many visitors up here. Are you lost?"

"I don't think so. I'm looking for a friend of mine. He appears to have gone off the trail," Hector answered. "We were to meet at the shelter."

"No one has wandered over here. You could be mistaken for a bear in that brown coat. That could get you shot in these woods."

"These must be his footprints though. They left off the trail before the shelter. They seem to go right to your cabin. Surely you saw him. His name is Sam Hanson."

"I'm afraid you are mistaken. Those are my prints. I went to the store yesterday evening and got caught in the snow. Let me show you back to the trail." Jolly walked away from the house and looked back.

"But there are two sets of prints coming to the house," Hector pressed. "I have no doubt one is yours coming back from the store. But what about the other set?"

"Ah. I dropped something and went back for it."

Sam set the computer back to where Jolly had left it and peeked out the front door. He could see Hector towering over Jolly. Hector pulled out a pistol and aimed it at Jolly.

"You don't seem to understand. If you had done that, there would be three sets of prints. No more stalling. If you will take me to Sam, you won't get hurt."

Jolly looked up to the sky and said loudly, "Thor help me!"

"Thor? Really?"

"Have you never heard of the Greek god? He is quite good at helping people."

Sam heard the back door open and looked back to see Thor squeezing out.

"It's time for us to go to the house. I'm eager to see that Sam is OK. Move."

Silent as light, Thor streaked through the snow, leaped, and landed his front feet on Hector's upper back. Hector fell forward, and before he hit the ground, Thor had his neck in a death bite.

"Hector Hoffman, meet Thor. As I said, he's quite adept at helping out."

Hector tried to get up, and Thor bit down harder. As Jolly fished Hector's gun out of the snow, Sam rushed out the front door with his gun aimed at Hector.

"Sam, I told you to hide," Jolly grumped. Then he chuckled. "I think we need a picture of this. The famous Hector Hoffman halted by a husky. Sam would you mind shooting him with your phone instead of your gun?"

Hector remained pinned on his belly, his face down in the snow. Thor eased the hold on his neck a little. Sam was flooded with emotions. He wanted to shoot Hector in the legs to make him suffer. He wanted to scream his rage. He wanted to demand that Hector take him to Evie. But he stood still, frozen by the conflict in his soul.

"Now what shall we do?" Jolly asked. "I suppose the best solution would be to let Thor finish the job. How do you feel about dying today, Hector?"

Jolly waited a moment. "Oh, yeah. You can't talk. If Thor kills you here, we will have to do something with your body. Not a pleasant thought. Sam, do you have any good ideas?"

A surge of rage ran through Sam. "I say let Thor have his fun. Then we'll drag the body to the trail. When someone finds him, they'll think he was killed by wolves. No questions asked."

Jolly gave Sam a long hard look, so long that Sam wondered what he was thinking.

"That's not very neighborly of you. Thor, stand down," Jolly finally said. "Before you get up, toss that knife and any other weapons over there."

Hector pulled the knife out of the case on his belt and threw it toward Sam, who quickly picked it up. Jolly checked the clip in Hector's Glock to make sure it was loaded and removed the safety. Thor growled as Hector lifted himself out of the snow. Sam realized what a large, powerful man Hector was.

"Let's all go into the house and get better acquainted," Jolly said.

"I'm afraid I have to go," Sam said. "There are things I need to do."

"Thor, ready. I can't let you do that." Jolly said. "I need you alive."

Thor circled around behind Sam, and Sam's nerves tightened. "If you have Hector, then I will be alive. We can send the police to verify what he has done and catch his bosses when they arrive."

"You don't get it, do you? The only thing Congress will respond to is death. The plan has to succeed. If the police show up, all Carter and Harrison have to do is say they learned about the abductions and came to rescue the victims. No one will question that and things go on just as they are. That is not acceptable I have come too far."

Sam turned his gun from Hector to Jolly. Jolly laughed loud and hard, then said, "Go ahead and shoot. I think you know what will happen. If Thor doesn't kill you, Hector will. Now let's go into the house where it's warmer and sort this all out."

Sam's heart nearly burst. He knew Jolly was right. And if he died, Evie and the others certainly would. His mind scrambled for options. "What if I shoot Hector," he thought. "That would eliminate one threat. It would also spoil Jolly's plans because there would be no one to kill them. Would Jolly kill me? If so, then Evie might never be found. Would he let them die if Hector and I were both dead? I'm going to kill Hector. I can't believe I'm about to shoot a man. But it's him or Evie."

Jolly must have read Sam's mind. By the time he took aim, Jolly was standing between him and Hector. Thor snarled as he raised the gun.

"Now, now. There will be no killing at my house."

The raven cawed loudly and landed on Sam's shoulder. He had forgotten about the bird. Thor stopped snarling. "What is it trying to tell me?" Sam thought. The bird flew and landed on the house as if it, too, could read his mind.

"OK," Sam said and stomped to the house. His mind was reeling, searching for a way out. He plopped down in the chair by the computer. Jolly pulled in the stool from the kitchen and then produced a folding camp chair. "Have a seat, Hector."

"OK, we are in a predicament," Jolly said. "Hector, you and I both need Sam alive to complete our missions. Unfortunately, you need him in one place, and I need him in another. Sam needs the two of us dead, well actually the three of us counting Thor, so he can save his wife. Hector, it looks like you and I are on the same team, but you were going to kill me. Sam is our common threat, yet he and I have guns trained on you. How did we get to this place?"

While Jolly was laying out the dilemma, Sam scrutinized Hector. Hector didn't look evil. Sam thought, "If I met you on the street, you would seem like a normal person. Rude, but normal!" It suddenly hit Sam that this was the man he had seen at the store.

"How do you know me?" Hector asked.

"Knowing stuff is what I do," Jolly responded.

"Why do you kill people?" Sam blurted out.

Hector looked at Sam. A little blood trickled down his neck from Thor's bite. He wiped it and looked at his hand. "It's a job that pays well."

"I don't see how you live with yourself. You kill innocent people who have done you no wrong."

"You're not innocent," Hector responded. "All of you have cost my bosses a lot of money, embarrassment, and headaches."

"Don't you have nightmares?"

"No. It's about right and wrong. Everyone I have taken out has wronged another person. I am simply making things right again."

"But we haven't done anything wrong. It is your bosses who did the wrong thing."

"Right versus wrong is simply a matter of perspective."

Sam exploded. "That's how you justify your horrific acts! I can't believe it! Don't you have a conscience? Is nothing sacred to you?"

Hector looked Sam in the eye. "You know, I think you are right. Come with me, and we will go set the others free."

"You would do that?" Sam asked as excitement and apprehension collided in his heart.

Jolly laughed. "And walk away from his big paycheck? He's lying."

"You should let Sam come with me. Then you won't get hurt," Hector said.

"You don't seem to understand. I have nothing to lose," Jolly replied. "My life ended a long time ago. The country, on the other hand, has everything to gain. I will be keeping Sam with me at all costs. You are free to go."

"That's not very hospitable of you," Hector replied. "You should at least offer me coffee after I walked this far to see you."

"You're right. How insensitive of me. I'll make some. Sam, shoot him if he gets up. Thor, guard."

Thor stood in his bed and glared at Hector.

"You don't have to go through with this, you know. You have a choice, and you could choose to do the right thing," Sam said.

"Right and wrong. Is that all you think about? There are so many shades of right and wrong. This seems wrong to you, but it seems right to my employers. I am just doing the job they hired me to do. It is how I have come to make a living."

"You're an evil person, and I hope you rot in Hell."

"If you shoot me, you can join me there."

"I think God would forgive me for ridding the world of you."

"But this is my last job. After today, I will be the good person you want me to be."

Rage boiled in Sam's blood. All he could see was Evie dying at this man's hands. "If Hector lives, Evie is sure to die. I'll gladly trade his life for hers," he thought and aimed the gun at Hector's heart.

"You can't pull the trigger."

"Watch me," Sam said. He squeezed the trigger. The millisecond before it fired, Thor snatched Sam's arm in his mouth.

Sam went down with the report of the pistol echoing in his ears. As his head hit the floor, he could see Hector running out the door, holding his shoulder.

Jolly ran into the room. "What have you done?" he yelled. He ran out the door and fired a shot at the fleeing Hector but missed.

Thor held Sam's wrist until he dropped the gun. As he started to get up, Jolly came back in.

"You idiot! Now he is out there and will surely be back to kill us both."

"But we have his weapons."

"Hector doesn't need weapons to kill."

Sam bent to pick up the gun he had dropped and Thor snarled.

"I think I'll be keeping that," Jolly said, scooping it up. "It's a bit of escape prevention."

Chapter 31

Hector ran until he saw a dense thicket of hemlock trees. He worked his way under them and pulled off his backpack. He located the small camping mirror before pulling his left shoulder out of his coat and shirt.

He rubbed the blood away with a handful of snow and examined the wound. "I've had worse," he said to himself, eyeing the laceration across his deltoid muscle. "I wish that dog had gotten there a split second sooner. At least it matches the other shoulder."

He pulled out the first aid kit and found antibiotic ointment, needle, and thread. He winced as he worked the needle through the raw edges of the wound. "I'm going to make sure you really suffer for this, Sam Hanson."

"It's not pretty, but it will do," he said studying his work. He got back into his shirt and coat and began plotting his next move. "That dog will make matters more complicated."

* * *

"I didn't think you would be the kind to actually kill a person. I can't believe you shot him. That was not in my plans," Jolly said glaring at Sam.

"Your plans! What exactly are your plans?"

"I told you. We use this tragedy to bring down the A-30."

"You're insane. You can't do that. But you can stop this tragedy!" Sam was yelling. Thor moved between him and Jolly.

"Thor says you need to calm down."

"Calm down! You must be loony! There is a killer out there who wants to kill my precious wife and friends, and you think I should sit here and sip coffee and enjoy the day!"

"I never said that. I said it would be a hard day. We have to make sacrifices. It is for the greater good."

"The last I heard, this is a free country. I need to go try to save my wife."

"You heard wrong. This is not a free country."

"I should be free to walk out of here if I want to."

"This country is in the noose of a few capitalists. No one is free. They determine everything. Ever since we elected one of them president thirty years ago and he changed the laws on monopolies, they have been amassing fortune and power. Now they control everything. They hire just enough people to run their businesses, imprison them in compounds, and let the rest of the country rot. You know that is true."

Jolly did not wait for a response. He sat on the floor and rocked and hummed.

"No! You don't get to just sit there and hum! We have to figure out a better way!" Sam shouted. He took a step toward the door, and Thor jumped in front of him. Sam fingered Hector's knife in his coat pocket.

Without a word, Jolly walked to a computer and began typing. After he was done, he growled, "Read!"

Sam moved to see the screen and read. It was an email addressed to Senator Alice Winston. "Senator Winston, I am aware that you share my concerns over the increasingly extreme behavior of the A-30 members. The intelligence regarding two of the A-30 members hiring an assassin to execute a number of people is very disturbing. I think it is time to rein in these corporations. I would be willing to explore possibilities with you. Sincerely, Jack Cheney, U. S. Senator."

Sam looked at Jolly, speechless.

"Senator Winston will not want to admit that she doesn't know about the intelligence that Cheney references. She will go along as if she is aware of it and start a conversation. I can prompt them toward the correct solution."

"Even if you could get the email delivered, they will see right through it. They will know it didn't originate through the government servers."

"You are wrong again. I have the ability to route this through their servers. If they bother to check for authenticity, which is unlikely, it will pass."

Remembering how Jolly had manipulated his phone, Sam entertained the notion that Jolly might be able to do what he said. "But still, even if you get two senators 'talking,'" he said making air quotes, "it doesn't mean anything will happen. There are children of the A-30 who are in the Senate. They won't let their parents' businesses be dismantled."

"I have fifty-four senators already discussing this. I have been seeking my revenge for a long time. This is the straw that will break the camel's back, so to speak."

"I thought you said revenge is devils' work."

"It is." Jolly pressed Send.

"You can do your email campaign without me. I need to go."

"I can't let you do that. It will bring down the whole endeavor if you leave."

"You can't stop me."

"You don't have a gun, but I do."

"I have a knife."

Jolly shot Sam a look that made Sam's blood chill. He sat on the floor and started humming.

Sam finally recognized the tune: "Stairway to Heaven."

Jolly kept humming and rocking.

"Would you stop already?" Sam said.

Jolly didn't respond. Sam stood staring at Jolly for a moment. Then his mind seized on the opportunity, and he took three tentative steps toward the kitchen. The humming continued. Jolly's eyes were shut.

Sam picked up his gun that still lay on the floor and quietly slipped out the back door, grabbing his coat as he went. Thor just watched as he passed, looking from him to Jolly and back.

Sam went with the first plan that crossed his mind and hurried behind the outhouse. He continued downhill, keeping the outhouse between him and Jolly's cabin. Sam cursed the snow as he went. "Anyone will be able to follow me." He stopped, remembering how Viviana had covered their tracks when leaving the cave.

He found a sturdy stick, retraced his steps, and smoothed over the tracks as best he could, trying not to rush and miss places. He continued until he was out of sight of the outhouse, expecting to see Thor coming after him any second. Sam remembered how the dog had attacked Hector and looked around to make sure he hadn't circled behind.

"That was too easy," he thought. He didn't linger. He turned and hurried, battling the deep snow and his nerves. He pushed on for what he guessed was half a mile before he was out of breath. He grabbed his knees and huffed and puffed.

As his breathing slowed, Sam tried to decide his next step. He tried to remember what he had seen on Jolly's screen. The crushing need to find Evie before it was too late made it hard for him to recall what he had seen.

"OK, I need options. I wish I had a piece of paper." He pulled out his phone and opened a blank document. "This will do."

He entered the first thought that crossed his mind, "How did Hector find me?"

He decided it would not be helpful to linger on that one, so he continued his list:

"Cut across the mountains?

Go back into town?

Call the police?"

"Wait," he thought and checked his phone for signal strength. "Nothing. So that option is out. I might get a signal if I got to the top of a mountain." Sam felt the pressure building. He checked the time on his phone. "It's already nine thirty-seven!"

Standing there thinking, he jumped at the crack of three gunshots. He crouched down and looked all around but could see no one. He went back to trying to decide what to do.

"I know where she is. I just have to decide the best way to get there. Cutting across the mountains looked to be the shortest route, but I may not be able to get through that way. If I go back into town, I can get the police to help me. Surely they will listen if I give them the coordinates."

Having made his decision, he looked around. "Which way is town? I know it is basically west, but which way is that?" Realizing what he had to do made Sam cringe with fear. "I have to use my GPS app." His finger was shaking as he opened the settings. "I hope it was Jolly doing the shooting," he said as he turned the GPS on.

Chapter 32

The sun came over the mountain, making the snow bright on the ridge across the way. Sam turned to block the glare so he could see his phone better. He studied the location to which he thought Hector had taken Evie. It was so much closer to go across country, but Sam feared he might not be able to find a way across the mountains.

"I'd better go into town and get the police." A sudden wave of longing flooded over him. "I want to see Evie." The longing collided with stress and fear. "I have to trust that she is OK," he said to himself. "I have to believe that I can save her. There is no other reality I can bear."

* * *

Evie's back felt bruised where Hector's knee had landed. Mostly she felt angry. "He can't get away with this," she said.

"He has so far," Sandi said. "No one is going to find us."

"Sam will," Evie said.

"How?" Sandi asked.

"I think he will be the next one Hector brings," Viviana said. "He said there was one more when he left you."

"There is no way Sam can elude this guy," David said. "He's a monster."

"I'm so hungry," Sandi moaned.

"You've been stuck here the longest. I'm so sorry Sandi," Evie said. "How long has it been since you've eaten?"

"I have no idea. Time is a blur."

"You said you had eaten the last of the bars the night before I was deposited," James said. "I remember you apologized for having nothing to offer."

"I think his plan is to let us all starve to death. The reason he is bringing Sam last is so he will have to watch the rest of us die. It's the cruelest thing he could do to Sam," Viviana pointed out.

"I wish I would just hurry up and die," Sandi said.

"Don't talk like that. We have to stay positive. We're going to get through this," Evie replied. "So there is nothing to eat. Do we have water?"

"There is about half a gallon left," James said, "but there is enough snow to last a long time."

"Viviana, do you think there are any acorns on the ground for us to eat? Or anything?"

"I haven't looked yet. The snow is so deep, it will be hard to find anything."

"It's hard to imagine how a human being could do this to fellow human beings. The depth of sin is hard to believe," David said.

"You might as well preach us a sermon. You have a captive audience," Viviana quipped.

Everyone laughed until they saw Sandi's tears.

"I just know we are going to be OK," Evie said. "Sam will find us."

* * *

Sam entered the location of the house where they had all stayed the night before and studied the directions the app provided. He set off, crashing through the snow and trees as fast as he could.

After half a mile, he was totally winded. He stopped and bent over with his hands on his knees, breathing as hard as he could. He wanted to hurry but knew he would never make it at that pace. Once he had caught his breath, he resumed at a pace he could sustain.

The app was leading him back to the trail. "If Hector is out there, that is probably where he would be. I think I'll go parallel to it as long as I can." He continued to fight through the snow and tree branches. It was hard going, but he felt safer until he heard the crack of a stick breaking.

Sam snapped his head in the direction of the sound. He could see nothing but hemlocks. He moved to the right and thought he saw brown. "That looks like the same color as Hector's coat," Sam thought. "It's the phone. He tracked my phone!"

He glanced at the direction back to town then turned off the GPS as quickly as his cold fingers could. Panic rose in Sam's heart, urging him to run. He looked down at his khaki-colored coat. "At least it's not bright orange."

He moved as quietly as he could behind a thick hemlock trunk and tried to slow his breathing. "I need options," he thought. "Running will surely give me away. I could stay here and hope he hasn't precisely located my phone."

Panic was making it hard to think. "Maybe I should turn the GPS back on and throw the phone into the woods to lead him away. But then I wouldn't have a phone or the coordinates. I could try to memorize them."

While he was trying to decide, he peeked around the trunk. A wolf was lumbering by about twenty yards away. It looked at him and sniffed, then continued on its way.

Sam scanned the area where he had originally heard the sound. The brown was gone. He breathed a deep sigh of relief. "Lesson learned," he thought. "No more GPS. At least until I'm ready to locate Evie."

He suddenly felt terribly alone. "I miss you, Evie. I need you to help me figure this out." A flutter of wings drew Sam's attention up the tree. The raven landed on a branch about ten feet up, knocking snow down onto his face. "Gee, thanks," he said as he brushed off the snow.

"I don't suppose you have any good ideas," he said to the bird.

It flicked its wings and bobbed its head silently. Sam's heart pounded. He could hear it beating in his ears. He pressed himself against the tree trunk then peeked around. He could see brown about forty yards away, moving slowly.

"Idiot! The wolf was gray!" he scolded himself. He pulled back behind the tree and listened carefully. He could barely hear the crunch of snow. Gradually the crunch got louder. Every fiber in Sam's body wanted to run, but he made himself stay still. He looked up at the raven. It was statue still.

Sam turned his attention away from the roaring of his heart back to the crunch of snow. He wasn't sure if it was wishful thinking, but the sound seemed to be getting farther away. He hardly breathed till he could no longer hear anything. He half expected to see Hector right next to the tree when he peeked around, but he saw nothing.

"OK, now what?" he thought. He looked up at the raven. It remained perfectly still. He interpreted the bird's posture to mean Hector was still close. He remained frozen in place while his mind and heart raced.

"I'm not moving until the raven does. But which way to go? Hector is ahead of me. I need to name this bird. What am I going to do next?"

Jumbled thoughts flew through his mind while he tried to settle on a plan. The raven was still not moving a feather. Sam quieted himself and thought, "What would Evie do?"

It was as if he heard her voice say, "Trust the bird."

"Trust the bird?" Sam whispered to himself. "I'm supposed to let a bird be in charge of saving my wife's life?"

The wisdom of the revelation settled into his heart, and he realized that was exactly what he needed to do. "You've gotten me this far," he thought. "I'll just wait and see what you suggest next."

He got cold as he stood still waiting. The raven didn't move, so he waited longer. His fingers and toes were getting numb. He waited some more. He looked at his watch, and it had been only twelve minutes.

He leaned against the tree trunk. "Maybe it is waiting for me to make a move." He decided to test this theory by starting to walk. He took four steps and looked up at the bird. It was bobbing its head and flicking its wings.

Sam crept back to the tree. "I guess that answers that question."

Almost imperceptibly, the sound of crunching snow began to register in his ears. "Hector's coming back," he cringed. The crunching got closer.

He tried to peer into the distance, but the hemlock branches blocked the way. The raven took flight and flew southwest toward town. Before Sam could figure out whether to stay put or follow, he heard loud caws. The caws moved farther away.

"Has it abandoned me?" Sam thought before he noticed the sound of crunching snow receding. "Could he be following the bird?"

He remained frozen in place and wondered, "Now what? It's hard to trust a bird that isn't here." Time seemed to freeze like Sam's fingers. He waited, his body getting colder and stiffer. "I need to get moving," he thought. "But if Hector catches me it's all over."

It was at that moment that he remembered his cold hand was wrapped around the handle of the gun. "I just need to see him before he sees me. I should have shot when I saw him. No, he was too far away. I never would have hit him."

Finally the raven returned, coming from the east. It landed on the same branch and resumed perching silently.

Sam looked at the bird, and it looked him in the eye. "Thanks," he whispered. His wonder at how the raven could possibly have figured out to do what it did supplanted his effort to plan his next move. While he was still pondering, the bird flew to a tree about twenty yards northeast.

Fear tightened Sam's chest. "Do I move or do I stay?" His mind said stay, but his gut said go. "Trust the bird." He set off toward the tree in which the raven perched.

The raven led him northeast toward town. The going was tough with the snow and no trail. Sam had to fight his way through branches, undergrowth, and rock outcroppings.

He came to a ten foot drop off down a huge rock and had to detour about forty yards to get past it. The raven seemed to wait patiently.

"At least we are going a different direction from Hector," he thought.

The snow thinned and then disappeared, making the walking easier. Then he came upon a creek swollen with water from the storm the night before.

Sam looked up, and the raven was on the other side. "I can't fly, you know. I need a break while I try to figure out how to get across this." He sat on a rock near the creek.

"I need a name for you. If I could get on the internet, I could look up a cool Tlingit name. I need to learn more of our language." Sam cringed when he realized he was talking out loud. "What if Hector heard?" he thought. He listened but could hear nothing over the roar of the creek. The raven seemed calm so he decided it was OK.

He went back to puzzling over a name. The raven cawed and flew back and forth between two trees. Sam sensed it wanted him to come on.

"OK, but I haven't thought of a name yet." He got up and studied the creek for a place to cross. He looked down river and saw a tree that had fallen. "Maybe it fell across the creek," he hoped. The leaves seemed fresh. "This must have fallen last night in the storm."

The huge oak did go across the creek, so Sam climbed up on it and began to make his way over. At first he had to fight his way through the branches. When he reached mid creek the branches stopped, leaving only trunk. He was about ten feet above the water.

A surge of fear hit as he looked down. He dropped to his knees and held tightly to the trunk. The raven cawed.

"That's easy for you to say. You can fly," Sam responded. He tried to go on hands and knees, but the bark dug in and hurt. He faltered to his feet. He could feel his heart pounding as he took tentative steps until he was back over land. He was almost close enough to the ground to jump off when the bark he stepped on gave way and he fell.

The raven chortled.

"Are you laughing at me?" Sam said as he rolled onto his back. He closed his eyes trying to assess whether anything beyond his pride was hurt. When he opened his eyes, an ancient woman was standing over him.

Chapter 33

Sam was startled when he saw the old woman and scrambled to his feet, slipping on his first try. The raven chortled again. He stared at the woman. Her face was wrinkled. Her long thick hair flowed down to her waist in two braids like rivulets of mist. Boots and blue jeans peeked out beneath an astonishing piece of clothing that he thought was a blanket. She looked frail, and Sam wondered how she got this far into the wilderness.

"Who are you?" Sam finally asked after their long silence.

The woman said nothing as she circled Sam.

"Your bird is an ancient being," she finally said, her voice old and raspy. "His name is Daséikw."

"Daséikw," Sam repeated, trying not to butcher the pronunciation. "What does that mean?"

"Breath." The woman circled Sam again. "You are lost and need guidance. Daséikw will provide."

"I'm not lost. I know where I am going."

"A man who denies the truth is the most lost."

Sam was exasperated by this stranger. He felt the urgency of time slipping by. "Well, the bird, Daséikw, seems to know where we are going, so I will follow him."

"Daséikw led you to me."

"Who are you," Sam asked again.

"I am Shaanáy."

"I know I should have learned the Tlingit language better. What does that mean?"

"Valley. The clan leader should know his people's language."

"You know who I am."

"Yes."

"How can you know me? I've never seen you before."

"There are ways of knowing beyond seeing."

"What are you wearing?"

"You do not recognize it? You have much to learn. This is a raven's tail robe."

Sam glanced at his watch. 10:47. " Your robe is beautiful and it's great talking riddles with you, but I have to try to save my wife and four other people. He looked up to the raven. "Daséikw, which way?"

The raven sat silently.

"Great," Sam said.

"A fool rushes to where he does not know."

"I don't mean to quibble, but I know where I'm going," Sam said, trying to keep his temper and to show respect. "I have the coordinates in my phone."

"Yes. You have a location. Knowing where one is going is more than the last point on the journey. It helps to know how to get there, to see obstacles in the path, to know the implications of one's choices."

"I can't make that choice."

"I see this choice of which you speak weighs heavily. It is a hard one."

"So you don't know everything."

"How can one person know everything? While choices seem to be yes or no, often there are more than two options. It is a matter of opening the heart to see deeper."

Sam's frustration at wanting to get on with his mission was being quelled by intrigue with this ancient woman.

"Where do you live?" he asked.

"That is an odd question. I don't live in a place. I live here," she said placing her hand over her heart."

The urge to get moving surged, and Sam asked, "Why did Daséikw bring me to you?"

"I think there is a lesson the chief must learn. You need to stop and look within before setting out on this quest. Let your heart show you what you need. You are hunting but are also hunted. You seek help, but whom can you trust? Not everyone is on your side. Your heart can help guide you. But you have to stop and look inside for that to happen."

Sam's anger flared. "You mean I wasted all this time for you to tell me to listen to my heart? I don't have time to sit around and meditate! I have to go! Good grief!"

"You will pay dearly if you fail to use your inner resources. It is a skill the chief must learn."

"Thanks for the advice," Sam replied sarcastically. "I guess you are staying with her," he directed to Daséikw then stomped off toward town. He heard an angry sounding caw and looked back. The raven was bobbing its head and flicking its wings.

Sam shook his head and continued walking. "Go. He will need you," he heard the woman say. He didn't look back again.

"Listen to my heart," he muttered. "I need to listen to my head. I have to think this thing through. I need to get to the police before Hector finds me."

Sam stopped in his tracks. "I am here because the police couldn't protect us." The realization sent a chill down his spine. He had an eerie feeling the old woman was right. "Maybe I do need to learn how to do what she suggested."

He turned around to go back and talk with her. She was gone. He looked through the tree trunks and branches and moved to get different sight lines. He didn't see her.

He looked up at Daséikw. "Where did she go?" The bird sat silently. Sam had a sinking feeling that he had missed an important opportunity. He found a rock and sat down.

"OK, how do I look inside? How do I hear my heart?" He sat and pondered for a few seconds. "I need to figure out what to do. If I go to the police, they will want to hide me. But they could send people to rescue Evie and the others. A team of officers would have a better chance than I do."

While that seemed to be the best idea, something in Sam's heart kept tugging against it. "Why does this not feel right? It sounds solid to me. Is it that I want to be the one to rescue Evie and be her hero? What really matters is that she is saved. OK, that is the plan. But how do I do it?"

Sam was lost in thought when Daséikw flew in his face, then back up into the tree. Sam looked up startled. The bird was flicking its wings and bobbing its head. "Uh-oh," Sam thought. On instinct, he hopped up onto the rock, grabbed the first branch of the tree, and pulled himself up. He climbed high into the tree and perched on a limb near Daséikw.

To the west, he could make out a patch of brown moving through the trees. Sam watched as the patch approached. It was definitely brown and not wolf colored. "He's doing a search grid from the coordinates my phone gave him," Sam thought. "The man doesn't give up. I'll have to remember that. This will be a good time to plan."

He tried to focus on figuring out what to do, but his fear of Hector kept him watching his movements. Hector passed about twenty yards south of Sam and continued east. Sam looked at Daséikw. He stood still. Sam waited and watched the brown coat proceed out of sight.

"Now I'm ahead of him. I need to hurry to beat him to town." He made a move to go down, then looked back at Daséikw. He glided out of the tree and flew west to the next tree. A wave of relief washed through Sam. When his feet hit the ground, he wanted to run but knew that would make too much noise. He forced himself to fox walk like Viviana had taught him and followed Daséikw as quickly as he could.

The pressure to elude Hector weighed heavily on Sam, and the weight seemed to transfer into his footfalls. It was hard to walk quietly when he felt in such a rush. "So much for listening to my heart," he thought.

Daséikw led him down the ridge and into a valley. A few passing clouds played tricks on the light coming through the trees. Sam cringed, knowing he would be more visible in the bright light.

He tried to guess how long he had before Hector turned back west. "I wonder when he will give up and assume I've gone on into Sitka?"

He stopped and looked over his shoulder, scanning the woods for the brown patch. He looked up to Daséikw. The bird had flown to the next tree and seemed to be urging him to hurry. He gladly obliged, following Daséikw till they came out on a trail.

The trail led them to the campus of Sitka High School.

"You just had to bring me back here," he said to Daséikw.

Chapter 34

Sam walked till he was hidden behind the building and stopped to plan. "What would Hector do?" he said to himself. Then he chuckled. "He's probably thinking, 'What would Sam do?'"

His next thought chilled his blood. "What if he finds my trail and is able to track me? I need to keep moving!"

Daséikw came flying really fast from the woods and landed at Sam's feet. The raven looked Sam in the eye then flew around the building.

Sam couldn't figure out how, but he knew Daséikw wanted him to follow and to move quickly. He suspected the urgency was that Daséikw had seen Hector coming. These thoughts worked through his mind as he raced around the high school in the direction Daséikw had flown.

He ran, dodging cars as he hurried through the parking lot to the front of the building. When he rounded the corner, he stopped dead in his tracks, and his blood chilled.

"What have I done?" he said, pulling at his hair. "I've led a killer to a school full of students!" Adrenaline surged as he tried to figure out what to do. "Shaanáy said to listen to my heart. My heart says run!"

Sam began to run south down Lake Street, toward Swan Lake. "I wish I could run like Evie," he thought as he began to huff and puff after a quarter of a mile. He stopped as another chilling thought registered. "Hector will assume I went into the school. He will go in looking for me. I have to do something to draw him away."

He pulled out his phone, feeling stressed. "That's the only way I can see to get out of this mess." He opened the picture he had taken of the locations he thought Evie was being held. Studying the photo he said, "It's either this house or this place in the mountains." He knew where the house was since it was just down the road from his own.

He pulled up the coordinates of the mountain location. "57°05'29.1"N 135°16'01.3"W." I'll never remember all of that. Maybe I can memorize the degrees and hours. "57 05. 135 16. 57 05. 135 16…." Sam said the numbers over and over as he turned on the GPS.

He pocketed the phone and began to trot. "I have a long way to go." He continued down Lake Street with Daséikw flying just ahead. Swan Lake came into view on the right. Sam continued along the street until he saw the little park, more like a pull-off really. A small dock protruded into the lake.

"I know what to do!" Sam thought and veered to the dock. Geese and ducks scattered as he ran. "They're expecting a treat," he thought. He set his phone on one of the benches. "Here is where you will find me, Hector. I'll be pondering life by the lake."

He cringed, seeing his phone on the bench, knowing he was going to leave it and cut off his access to the world… to help. He looked north, scanning for a brown coat but saw nothing. "I wonder how far away he is," he thought as he resumed his jog. He headed south on Lake Street, reached the roundabout, and stopped. "Now which way?"

An urgent caw pierced Sam's thoughts. He looked back and saw brown turning into the park where he had stashed his phone. Even though Hector was almost a quarter of a mile away, Sam could tell that he had seen him. For some reason, he stood and watched while Hector picked up his phone.

Urgent caws finally brought Sam out of his paralysis. He ran in Daséikw's direction, running as hard as he could. He looped around the end of the park and headed north on Halibut Point Road.

* * *

Hector paused and watched as Sam ran. A slow smile spread across his face. "You are mine." He kicked at a goose that had come close, took two steps, then stopped. Hector looked at the phone for a second, then threw it into the middle of the lake. "Just in case the police want to find you." He looked south just in time to see Sam disappearing around the corner. "I do love a good chase. This guy is proving to be a worthy opponent." He said aloud, "But you will never escape."

* * *

Sam dashed up Halibut Point Road then noticed Daséikw had flown to the left down Erler Street. Sam dodged a couple of cars as he crossed the road, cut across the bank's parking lot, and caught up with Daséikw. The bird cawed and flew on. A hill with a forest rose to the left of the road.

Suddenly Daséikw veered and flew down a trail. Sam looped and came back to the trail. "Great," he thought as he read the sign. "The Russian Orthodox Cemetery. Just what I need."

A gate blocked the path. Sam turned and pushed through the undergrowth and around the gate. He followed Daséikw into the dense woods. A root snagged his toe before his eyes adjusted to the shadowy darkness, and he crashed onto the trail. Popping back onto his feet, he discovered a scraped knee and small scratches on the heels of both hands.

"No time to worry about that," he thought as he raced after Daséikw. He came to an intersection of trails and for the first time noticed the grave markers nestled in the undergrowth. Stopping to decide which way to go, Sam noticed an eerie quietness. Daséikw had disappeared.

He thought he heard footfalls in the distance, someone running. "Idiot!" he thought. "He can track me on this trail." His heart began racing. "Where is that bird when I need him?"

He found a fallen branch, ran a few feet ahead, then started backing and wiping away his footprints. He carefully tiptoed back to the intersection, stepping in his own prints, then took the trail to the west, continuing to erase his prints. The footfalls were getting closer, and he struggled to keep wiping away his prints rather than turning and running.

After about a hundred feet, he tossed the stick and ran. He felt the brush of wind as Daséikw flew right over his head. The bird veered to the left, and Sam followed him along a rock ledge. The bird landed beside a huge hemlock with a large hole in its base that dropped underground.

"No way! I'm not going in there." He could hear the sound of running feet getting closer. "Trust the bird," he seemed to hear Evie say. He gathered his courage, then slid into the hole and underground.

Darkness collided with the dank, damp smell of earth as Sam descended. About eight feet down, the narrow tunnel opened into a cavern large enough for him to stand. "Great. If he kills me here, no one will ever find me. At least they won't have to worry about burying me."

He tried to distract himself from his fear by exploring the cavern. Touching the wall, he found a mix of dirt, roots, and rocks. He stepped on something that crunched. He couldn't bring himself to reach down to see what it was.

He followed the wall with his fingers and was able to walk about eight feet before coming to an end. He could see the light coming in from the tunnel that led out. A wave of fear surged through him. He wanted to get out of that hole but knew he didn't dare.

He leaned against the wall of the cavern and tried to figure out how Hector had followed him. "I understand how he could have found my trail in the woods, but how could he know I turned up Erler Street? There are no footprints on asphalt. Oh, maybe he could have seen me through the trees. Then it would have been easy to see where I went around the fence. If I get out of here, I will have to be more careful."

Thinking helped ease the fear coursing through Sam's veins, but he couldn't shake the feeling of being trapped. It took all he had to stay down in the cavern. "Surely he won't come down here," he thought as he settled in to wait.

"What is that sound? Must be wind catching at the mouth of the cavern. I have to focus. I need to come up with a plan for when I get out of here."

He tried to concentrate on how to get to the house from which Evie had been abducted. "I wonder if they moved to another location. Maybe I should try to get to the police station. But what if they are all out searching?"

In the quietness of the cavern Sam could hear air moving but felt no breeze. The sound was coming from his left, farther back in the cavern, not from the entrance. It dragged him out of his thoughts. "Breath. Something is breathing!"

Sam heard Daséikw caw in the distance. "I'm not falling for that again," drifted down into the cavern. Hector's voice. "He's close."

It sounded like Hector was just outside the hole. Sam moved to his left so that he wouldn't be seen if Hector shined a light down into the cavern. The sound of breathing got closer. Sam's foot hit something heavy.

He bent down to feel what it was. "A bear's paw! Great!" Sam's fear escalated three more notches. Then he jumped when light hit the wall of the cavern, shining down from above.

"You can come out now. I know you're down there," Hector called.

Chapter 35

Hector's words sent a shockwave through Sam. "He'll come down here," Sam thought.

"Don't make me come after you," Hector called.

Sam didn't say a word. He listened carefully to the breathing of the bear. "That must have been a front paw I touched." He moved his left foot gently. Feeling no bear parts, he stepped. He continued till he touched something. It was the other wall of the cavern.

"I don't have all day," Hector called down into the hole.

Sam felt and found the bear's rump. It was nearly to the wall. He squeezed by the bear, keeping his hand on its rump to prevent himself from falling onto the bear. The bear stretched, and Sam froze.

"Good grief," Hector said.

Sam heard the scramble of rock sliding as Hector began his way down the hole. Sam pushed past the bear quickly, and it rolled off its side. Sam followed the side of the cavern with his fingers. It turned. There was a recess behind the bear.

He scurried into the recess, which led him down into another cavern. He could hear Hector sliding down into the cavern he had just left. He saw Hector's light and could make out the shadow of the bear.

"Oh, crap!" he heard Hector yelp, followed by scrambling that he assumed was Hector hustling out of the cavern.

Sam could just make out the shadow of the bear against the light coming down the hole. It stood, turned, and lay back down.

"Great. Now what?" Sam thought as he stared at the mound of bear between him and the exit. "I guess I have to wait long enough to be sure Hector is gone, then climb back over the bear."

He pushed on the backlight of his watch. 12:06. Stress surged in his soul. "I have less than five hours!" He paced, hands outstretched to keep from running into anything. After twelve steps (he counted them), he hit his head on a rock protruding from the ceiling.

"I think I'd better sit down." He moved back to the wall where he could see the outline of the bear, sat down, and leaned back. It was noticeably warmer in the cavern than the chill of outside. Fatigue from stress and lack of sleep ebbed into Sam's body.

"I need to stay here thirty minutes to give Hector time to move on. That's 12:36." He got warm and comfortable. "I can't go to sleep," he thought and shook his head. He thought about a plan. "Since I don't know where they might be, I think I had better go straight to Evie. Maybe I can beat Hector there."

Images of running down the streets he would take to get to Evie turned to mist, then faded. Sleep took Sam to another place.

He was trying to run in deep snow. His legs were so heavy he could hardly move them. It took all his effort to make one difficult step at a time. A pounding sound was coming up behind him. He had to get away but could barely move. The sound was getting closer.

Bears and wolves came thundering up and passed him. The thundering sound was still coming. It was getting louder. He kept trying to run, but his feet were like lead weights. Up ahead, one bear had stopped. It was standing on its hind legs and looking at Sam.

Sam looked back. An avalanche was crashing down the mountain and heading his way. He knew he would be crushed if he didn't run, but his legs were so heavy. His heart pounded, and he knew he was about to die. The bear continued to stare.

Just as the avalanche was about to bury him, Sam startled himself awake. He jumped, confused, looked around wanting to run but not sure why or where. He remembered the dream, then slowly realized where he was. He could still see the mound of the bear.

He panicked and looked at his watch. 12:44. "Wow. I slept eight minutes too long. I still don't have a plan, though." Sitting in the darkness of the cave, he pondered. The nap helped to sharpen his thinking.

"I need to figure out what Hector would do so I can evade him. He's looking for me, so where would he think I'm going?"

A sinking feeling hit Sam in the gut when this thought came: "I could have texted the coordinates to Grandpa before I left the phone." He slapped himself on the forehead. "Why didn't I think of that? I'm an idiot, that's why!" Realizing his mistake left him paralyzed.

"Maybe this was the avalanche," he thought. "Dwelling on my screw-up will not save Evie. I have to focus on what I can do, not on my failure." He wrenched his mind back into gear. "What would Hector expect me to do? What would he do when he couldn't find my tracks?"

Sam tried to see through Hector's eyes. He pictured himself looking around where he last saw tracks. "I'd look up in the trees. Then I think I would assume that I kept going. But where would I go? Does he know that I know where Evie and the others are? He could have seen the picture on my phone."

Sam felt the weight of another sinking thought. "He could tell that I haven't called or texted anyone to let them know what's going on."

He felt the paralysis slipping back in. "I have to focus. What would I do if I were Hector? Since I don't know where the guy I'm hunting has gone, would I assume he is going back to the house? To the police? Straight to Evie? A car! Hector probably has a car somewhere. Would he go back to that?"

* * *

Hector was breathing hard after scrambling to get away from the bear. He looked around for tracks but found none. He looked up into the trees but saw no Sam. He did see Daséikw sitting in a tree looking down at him. He wondered if it was the same raven that had led him astray before. He glared at the bird, and the bird glared back.

Hector had an eerie feeling. He couldn't quite put his finger on what was leaving him shaken. It seemed the bird could see right through to what he was thinking. He looked away from the bird but sensed it was still watching him. He looked back up. The raven's eyes were still locked on him.

"This is ridiculous," he thought. "It's just a black bird in a cemetery. I'm Hector Hoffman. A bird can't scare me." He tried to shake the creepy feeling. "I have to get back to hunting my prey. Now, if I were Sam Hanson, what would I do? If I'm running from a person trying to kill me, where would I go? But that's not all. He's not just trying to get away from me. He wants to save his wife. Could he know where she is?

"Stupid! Stupid! Stupid! I should have kept his phone!" he said smacking himself on the forehead. "It might have told me if he had found the shelter. Where could this guy have gone? I have to assume I have just lost his trail. Maybe he covered it up better than his usual scratching." He stopped and listened but heard nothing but distant traffic.

He looked around at the old graves and old trees. "This would be a nice place for a picnic. But I have no time to dally. What to do? What to do? I think I need my Jeep. I could cover more ground with it." He looked back up at the bird. It was gone. The creepy feeling was back. "I need to get out of here."

He called for an Uber and retraced his way to Erler Street. He twisted his neck to check the hole made by Sam's bullet. "A little blood but not bad. Maybe the driver won't notice."

* * *

The urge to get moving was strong, but Sam didn't want to leave the cavern without a plan. "I'm near the police station. That might be the first place Hector would expect me to go."

He puzzled a little more before a plan started to emerge. "I'll do what he doesn't expect. I'll go the opposite direction and loop around to the south." His heart settled on the plan, and he decided to go. "Now to get past this bear."

He started up the steep grade and cringed when his foot slipped and rocks skittered down. The bear didn't move. He continued on hands and knees, rocks digging in sharply, till he got to level ground. The bear sat up, sniffing. Sam froze. The bear was blocking his path.

The bear moved to its right and looked at Sam. Sam didn't dare move, standing still as a statue. Daséikw flew down into the cave cawing loudly. He landed in front of the bear. The two eyed each other, then Daséikw cawed as if he were talking to the bear. The bear made a soft sound and sat down.

Sam couldn't believe his eyes. Drowsiness suddenly weighed him down and an overwhelming urge to sit and think came over him. He sat down and closed his eyes. He could smell the pungent odor of the bear and the soft dankness of earth. He wanted to get up but couldn't seem to make his body move.

He shook his head, wondering if there could be a gas in the air making him drowsy. He felt like he could understand Daséikw and the bear's conversation. Daséikw was explaining to the bear what Sam had to do. Even though his eyes were closed, he saw Shaanáy̓ standing next to the bear. "Listen to your heart," she whispered. Sam's dad appeared next to her. "I am proud of you, son. You can do this."

One by one ancient men appeared in the cavern, all wearing the same hat and blanket that Skauty had passed on to him. Without a word, they came and touched him on the shoulder. Sam looked each one in the eye and could feel the weight of their hands.

He wondered why he wasn't afraid. When he looked again, Skauty had his hand on his shoulder. "There is no need to fear. You are surrounded by the spirits of the chiefs of the past. They will guide you. The earth and its creatures are your friends. Love them, and they will love you. You will overcome this challenge."

The cavern began to clear till Shaanáý was the only one left. "See what happens when you listen?" Her voice lingered in the air, then she turned to mist and was gone.

Sam opened his eyes to find Daséikw and the bear watching him. Daséikw cawed and flew out of the cave. Sam stopped in front of the bear. "Thank you," he said and followed Daséikw.

As he came out of the earth, Sam felt a new power. His fear and anxiety were replaced with purpose. Doubt turned to certainty. Daséikw cawed, and he seemed to understand what the bird said.

"Yes, I want to go west because I think Hector will be looking for me in the east," he told Daséikw. The raven cawed agreement. Sam set off to save his people.

Chapter 36

Keeping a wary eye out for Hector, Sam made his way out of the cemetery by a path that led west. He could see traffic ahead as he approached Marine Street. A gray Jeep Gladiator passed, and the hair on Sam's neck stood up. "There's something not right about that Gladiator," he thought.

He came out on Marine Street and looked carefully for Hector. Not seeing him, he turned south, crossing the street so he could get on the sidewalk. He walked quickly but resisted the urge to run, knowing he needed to save his energy.

He could see Seward Street up ahead when the hair on the back of his neck stood up again. He looked back, and the gray Gladiator was coming his way. Sam was puzzled, but somehow he knew Hector was in that vehicle. "It must be the elders," he thought as he broke into a run.

He nearly ran into a car as he crossed Seward Street and took the next right down Barracks Street. He could feel the car getting closer but didn't dare turn to look.

He flew past a building that had been the newspaper office, cut left, and hid behind an old dumpster. He heard a vehicle pull into the parking lot. He peeked out and saw the back of the Gladiator as it pulled out the other side of the lot and turned right.

Sam waited, wondering what to do. He peeked again, and the car was out of sight. "I think my best bet is to go where he has already been." He sprinted across the parking lot to the cover of the next building and made his way to the street where he last saw the Gladiator.

At the corner he peeked around the building. The Gladiator was sitting in the road. His eyes met Hector's. When the car lurched backward in Sam's direction, he broke across the street, turned left away from the vehicle, ran through a couple of yards and hid in a grove of trees.

The gray Gladiator crept by on the road, and Sam pulled himself behind the trunk of the tree, panic growing with every heartbeat. Daséikw cawed from a tree to Sam's south. Without stopping to think, he ran in that direction.

Slashing through the rest of the grove, he came out between two buildings. He could see St. Michael's Cathedral across the way. Daséikw cawed from the top of the onion dome. Sam hesitated, looking carefully for the Gladiator. Not seeing it, he hurried inside the cathedral.

His sense of panic heightened when he didn't see a way out except by the doors through which he had entered. An elderly man came up. "Welcome to St. Michael's. Can I offer you a tour of the building?"

The man was pudgy with white hair and no teeth, his face and neck quite wrinkled. A light of recognition flickered in his eye. "You're Sam Hanson, our new chief. It is an honor to have you come by to visit St. Michael's. I'm Robin Talloaks," he said, holding out his hand.

Sam shook hands with him. "It's nice to meet you, too, Mr. Talloaks. Is there a way out other than the front door?" As he asked, he spotted doors to the side that were blocked and barred.

"There are doors over there," Robin pointed. "But they are locked and never used. We have to have them in case of a fire. You're not a fire inspector, are you?" he asked, seeming suddenly nervous.

"No, no. Just wondering," Sam said as he scanned the sanctuary trying to figure out what to do if Hector walked through the door.

"I see you have been doing yard work… or something," Robin said.

Sam looked down and realized how dirty he was. "Sorry, I didn't realize I had gotten so dirty. I think I'll sit and pray if that's OK."

"Of course. Just let me know if there is anything I can do." Another group of tourists came in, and Robin shuffled over to them.

Sam looked over the sanctuary. The ornate gilding and elaborate art work were beautiful and inspiring. He hadn't been in the sanctuary since a school field trip. He took one of the chairs that seemed randomly placed around the sanctuary. When he looked up, the Jesus icon was looking back at him from the cross. "Lord, help me," he prayed. "I have to figure a way through this."

He studied the figure for a bit, then closed his eyes. "I need to think like Hector. What will he do? What would I do?" He pondered for a minute. "He seems to be riding in circles. I guess he knows I will be on the street somewhere."

He ran his fingers through his hair and felt dirty. "How long has it been since I showered?" he wondered. "I have to focus. If I didn't see me on the street after a while, I would assume I was hiding. Would I get out of the car or keep driving in circles? Eventually I would run out of gas."

He looked back at the figure of Jesus. "You sacrificed your life for us," he thought and a flood of guilt washed over. "What if Jolly was right?" He cringed. "No. I can't do that. I would give my life for them, but I can't give their lives for mine. That is just not going to happen."

As the guilt receded, rage took over. He put his hand in his pocket and felt the gun. "Maybe I should go out, let him find me, then shoot when he gets near. That might work if he still wants to take me alive. He will probably try to tase me."

As his plan formed, Sam's rage receded into determination. He looked up at Jesus. "You may not like this, but I see no other way."

"Welcome to St. Michael's. Can I offer you a tour?"

"No, thank you. I am looking for a friend of mine."

Those words hit Sam's ears, and the whole world seemed to freeze. "Hector." Sam's body went stiff. He dared not look up, but he had to. His eyes met Hector's.

"There you are. I thought I would find you here," Hector said in a sickeningly friendly tone.

Sam didn't understand, but a boldness came over him. He looked at Jesus one more time, stood, and crossed over to Hector. "You were right. Here I am," Sam said.

"My car is waiting. Are you ready to go?"

Sam felt the gun in his pocket. "I can't shoot him in a church," he thought. "I'll have to wait till we get outside."

Then he said, "I have a message for you from the elders. You will not get away with this. You will be defeated."

"When you see the elders again, you can explain how they were wrong. Let's go."

"I have a feeling the elders were right," Sam said and looked Hector in the eye with a confidence born of his encounter in the cave.

The door opened for another set of tourists, and Daséikw burst in with an unkindness of ravens cawing and flying straight at Hector's face. While Hector tried to fend them off, Sam bolted out the door.

He turned left at the door, left at the street, and ran. After two blocks he saw Hector's car on the right. Just past the car he stopped and turned around. He grasped the gun but left it in his pocket. "I want him to get close."

Sam waited and watched. Hector came flying around the building with ravens attacking his head. He pulled out a pistol and shot into the air. The birds backed off. Hector looked up and smiled when he saw Sam.

"You have finally seen the light," Hector called as he closed the distance toward Sam.

"I have," Sam called back. "This has to end. I'm not going to let you kill my people."

Before Sam finished talking, Hector had his pistol and taser aimed at Sam. He kept coming. Sam noticed Daséikw diving. He stood still, bracing for the right moment.

Daséikw's talons caught Hector in the face. Hector twisted and covered his face with both hands. As he straightened back up, Sam saw a trickle of blood before he shot.

The blast knocked Hector backwards, and he sprawled on the sidewalk. The few people on the sidewalk yelled for help. One rushed to aid Hector. Sam turned and ran.

As he ran past buildings and dodged a couple of people on the sidewalk, Sam thought, "Maybe I should have stayed and waited on the police to get there."

He stopped and considered going back, but something inside urged him to keep running. He seemed to hear Shaanáý say, "Listen to your heart." He ran along Lincoln Street until he came to the intersection with Lake Street. Without thought, he ran into the street. A horn honked and tires screeched.

Sam waved a sheepish, "Thank you," and kept running. He was out of breath by the time he ran past the Bishop's House. Bending over with his hands on his knees, he huffed and puffed and tried to catch his breath. "Why am I running?" he thought.

He jumped when he noticed a car had stopped on the road next to him.

"Sam?" Joe said as the window rolled down.

Sam looked up and relief surged into his heart. "Am I glad to see you!"

"Get in. I have to respond to a shooting just down the road."

Sam opened the passenger door and slid in. "I'm afraid I'm the shooter. I shot Hector."

"Who is Hector?"

"He is the assassin who abducted everyone. And I know where he is holding them."

"Hallelujah!" Joe said. "Let's get this call over with and go get them. Of course, I may have to book you first."

Joe pulled up behind an ambulance. The doors were closed. Sam could see the driver talking to two people. There was no body on the sidewalk. There was also no blood.

"That's odd. They wouldn't move the body before I had a chance to examine the crime scene. Maybe they have him loaded in the ambulance," Joe wondered.

"If he weren't dead, why wouldn't they be headed to the hospital?" Sam asked.

"Sit tight while I have a talk with the witnesses."

Sam watched as Joe approached the driver. She shrugged her shoulders and lifted her palms. After a couple of minutes, Joe came back to the car.

"Hector got up and walked away. Are you sure you hit him?"

"Definitely. It knocked him to the ground."

"Kevlar," Joe said.

Chapter 37

Driving away from the scene, Joe said, "So this assassin is still on the loose. We will need backup to go to the location where you think the others are being held."

"He's driving a gray Jeep Gladiator," Sam said, craning his neck to see if he saw it. He shuddered when he realized that Joe had parked in the same spot where Hector's vehicle had been.

"Where have you been hiding?" Joe asked. "We've looked everywhere."

"I went to see Jolly."

"Jolly?"

"Yeah. He's Solar Wind, the one who has been sending those messages. He lives up the mountain off the grid. He has this wild idea that he can bring down the A-30 and restore America to the way it was."

Sam quickly ducked down below the dash. "Gray Gladiator to the left," he said.

Joe saw the Gladiator coming to a stop up ahead on Monastery Street.

"I wouldn't try to arrest him by yourself," Sam said. "He will probably kill you."

"How about with your help?" Joe asked.

"Oh, yeah. The two of us might do it."

Joe flipped on the blue light and pulled in front of the Gladiator, blocking the road. Before he could get stopped, the Gladiator wheeled around and flew up Monastery Street.

Joe backed up so he could pursue Hector.

"Stop," Sam said. "It's a trap."

"What do you mean? I need to arrest him."

"He will be blocking the road. He'll shoot you and take me."

"You can't know that."

"See Daséikw in the road?"

"Daséikw?"

"The raven in the street who is yelling at you."

Daséikw was in the middle of the street, cawing maddeningly.

"He won't let you pass," Sam said. "It's a trap."

Sam watched the expression on Joe's face as he looked from Sam to the bird and back. Sam could tell Joe thought he was crazy. Sam was addled himself and wondered how he could know something he couldn't see. But he was certain that Hector had his vehicle crossways in the road waiting for them to come.

Joe hesitated. "OK, I'll listen to you and the bird. Now what?"

"Let's go get Evie and the others. We need to get there before he does. From what I understand, he plans to kill everyone at five o'clock."

"From what you've been telling me, we will need more firepower than you and me."

"Well call already!" Sam barked.

Joe pulled out his phone and called Bryant. "Hey, Bryant. I found Sam, and he thinks he knows where the victims are being held… Yes, we need as many officers as you can muster. We are definitely dealing with a hired assassin… OK, I'm bringing Sam to the house, and we'll go from there."

He disconnected and said, "Bryant will gather people to go with us."

Sam looked at his watch and a surge of panic quickened every nerve in his body. "It's two twenty-five! I only have two and a half hours to save them! Drive!"

Joe pulled the car out and headed down Lincoln Street.

"You missed the turn," Sam huffed when Joe passed Baranof Street. "That was the shortest way."

"I don't want this guy to be able to follow us." He kept going, turned left at Finn Alley, and worked his way through the neighborhoods until he came out on Sawmill Creek Boulevard.

Sam opened the door before the car stopped and ran into the house from which Evie had been abducted.

"You're a sight for sore eyes," Skauty said and jumped up to hug his grandson.

"Where's Bryant?" Sam said as he briefly returned the hug.

"He's around here somewhere."

"Bryant!" Sam called, and Bryant strolled in from the kitchen, coffee mug in one hand and pocketing his phone with the other. Joe came through the door.

"Sam thinks he knows where the captives are being held," Joe said.

"It's about time we had a break," Bryant responded. "Where are they?"

"It looked like it was up Indian River Trail on the side of The Sisters Mountain. I had the coordinates, but I lost my phone trying to get away from Hector. I'm trying to remember them."

Sandra rushed into the room. "Oh, my God! I thought we had lost you!" She grabbed Sam in a hug.

"I'm OK, Mom."

There was a loud caw at the door. Sam opened it, and Daséikw flew in and landed on Sam's shoulder.

"Wow! Who is this beauty?" Skauty asked.

"This is Daséikw. He is helping me."

"My goodness," Sandra said and backed away a couple of steps. Daséikw flew to Skauty's shoulder as if they were old friends. Bryant walked over and reached out to pet Daséikw. He gave an angry caw, and Bryant stepped back.

"Not the friendliest bird, is he," Bryant said.

Sam's heart calmed. It felt good to be back with his people. But the drive to save his wife and his friends wouldn't let him be still.

Daséikw cawed and flew to a chair by the door.

"He's here," Sam said. "We need to get everyone into the kitchen now!" Sam started hurrying his mom and Skauty toward the kitchen. Glass in the front window exploded and a smoke bomb landed on the floor.

Joe was the last one in and slammed the door against the rising smoke. He grabbed Sam and shoved him toward the back door. "We have to get you out of here," he said. He looked out the back window, then opened the door and shoved Sam out. Sam nearly tripped down the steps from the push.

"Move!" Joe urged when Sam stopped and looked back at the house. Daséikw cawed from a tree to the south. It was then that Sam knew Joe was right. He turned to run and heard the sound of the front door being kicked in.

"I have to go back," Sam said, stopping again.

"Gary, Jordan, and Bryant can take care of the others. We have to keep you out of his hands so move," Joe urged.

They ran with Sam following Daséikw's lead. They crossed the road, ran past a house and into the woods. Two gunshots rang out just as they got into the woods. Sam froze again.

"There is nothing we can do. We have to trust that it was one of our folks shooting," Joe said. "We have to trust them and keep moving."

Daséikw added a caw of approval. Sam sensed that Joe was right. He stood silently, processing the emotions churning in his heart.

"There are three officers and only two shots were fired," Sam said. "That means they either shot Hector or surrendered. If they surrendered, Hector would leave and look for me. That means we are doing exactly what he would expect. We need to go back to the house. That's the last thing Hector would expect. Come on," he said and turned south, pushing through the woods.

Daséikw scolded and flew north. Sam paused. He had learned to trust the bird. Sam battled the inner conflict for only a second. He had made his decision. He was going back to the house.

He led Joe a little way south, then turned west, back toward the road. They peeked out from the trees, searching for any sign of Hector. Seeing none, they crossed the road and headed back toward the house, using the sparse foliage for cover as best they could.

Sam sidled up to the house and peeked into the living room window. The smoke was clearing, and the door was still open. No one was in there, so he moved to the kitchen window. They were all milling around, not looking worried.

He tried the door. It was locked, so he knocked. "It's Sam and Joe," he said quietly. The door didn't open. Joe knocked on the window and waved. Bryant cracked the door, gun at the ready, and looked around. Then he opened it and let them in. Daséikw scolded one more time as he flew in with them.

"What is your bird fussing about?," Bryant asked.

"We heard gunshots. What happened? Is everyone OK?" Sam asked, ignoring Bryant's question. He didn't want to admit that he had gone against Daséikw's advice.

"I shot twice into the smoke. Then we didn't hear anything," Bryant explained. We finally opened the door, and he was gone. I didn't see any blood but didn't spend a lot of time looking because of the smoke. I don't know if I hit him."

"He's wearing Kevlar," Joe said.

"Now what do we do?" Jordan asked.

"I say the five of us go after Evie and the others," Sam said. "We have to hurry."

"That's too risky," Joe countered. We need to leave at least two officers here to protect the others. Did you get any backup?" Joe asked looking at Bryant.

"Yes. Five officers should meet us at the Indian River trailhead in thirty minutes," Bryant said looking at his watch.

"Good," Joe said. "I'm going to the office to get rifles and ammunition. I think we'll need everything we've got to take this guy down."

"You are right about that. Hector Hoffman is an internationally known assassin. Jolly says he has never failed a mission," Sam explained.

"Jolly?" Bryant asked.

Sam explained, "He is Solar Wind. He's a hermit living up on a mountain. He says Mitch Carter and Holmes Harrison hired the assassin. Jolly has this crazy idea that he can use the deaths of the..."

He paused. He couldn't bring himself to say, "victims." Finally he got out, "Hostages to bring down the A-30. His plan was for me to wait with him until they were dead, then he would convince Congress and the President to dismantle the stranglehold the A-30 has on America."

"He sounds like a real nutcase," Bryant said. "I'm glad you got away from him."

"I think I'll bring a couple of assault rifles, too," Joe said.

Chapter 38

Joe started toward the front door but stopped. "Wait, we need to know where we are going. Sam, were you able to remember the coordinates?"

Sam tried to remember them, but they had faded. He closed his eyes and tried to picture the numbers on the phone. He saw only a blank screen. "I guess I forgot them with all that has gone on since I gave up my phone."

"What do you mean, you gave up your phone?"

"It's a long story, but I had to use it as a decoy to get away from Hector. Can someone pull up a map of The Sisters?"

Phones popped out of every pocket except Sandra's and Skauty's. Jordan had the map pulled up first.

Sam took her phone and studied the terrain. "I'm sure it is in this area," he said. He moved the map around to the houses at the end of Indian River Road. "I think he was staying at this house," he said pointing to the house he had seen on Jolly's computer.

"Let's check there before we head up the trail," Joe said. "Anyway, I'll meet you at the end of Indian River Road in twenty minutes."

Bryant opened the door right after Joe left. "I'm going to make sure our backup is on the way."

"I don't think I can wait twenty minutes," Sam said. He started pacing.

Bryant popped back in. "Why don't you and I go ahead so we will be ready when the others arrive?"

"I'm ready," Sam said, relieved to be moving. Thoughts of Evie being tied up somewhere haunted his heart.

* * *

Hector smiled as he closed out the text on his phone. "I'll have to hustle," he said to himself, noting the time on his watch. "It's three seventeen. I will be late, but not by much. He should be walking up just a little after five."

Hector drove in a hurry to the house, parked the car in the garage, and ran in. He stuffed what he wanted to take with him into a backpack. The rest he crammed into a garbage bag and put it into the outside bin. He made one last check to see that nothing incriminating was left behind.

Last of all, he carefully placed his signature on the kitchen counter. "This may be the last time I do this," he thought. He stood and admired the intricately carved cornflower. Carved in walnut and finished with tung oil, the flower was gorgeous.

"I must leave you, my precious. Maybe I will go back to Germany someday."

* * *

"Remember, the assassin may come back when he doesn't see Sam out on the road. Stay alert and don't leave your post," Bryant cautioned Jordan and Gary."

"Roger that," they said at the same time.

"Are you armed?" Bryant asked, looking at Sam.

"Yes," he said and held up his pistol.

"OK. Let's go." Bryant led the way to the front door, the smoke nearly having cleared. "Lock this behind us," he called back. They got into Bryant's rental car and drove toward the trailhead.

Sam had an uneasy feeling. Something wasn't right. He sensed he was heading into a trap. "I'm just stressed," he thought. He looked over at Bryant driving the car and felt distrust. "This is ridiculous. We are going to save Evie and my friends. There will be plenty of help to take on Hector."

He remembered how Daséikw had cawed when Bryant walked up to him. "Why would he do that?" His heart clouded with doubt.

"Listen to your heart," Sam seemed to hear. He looked up to see if Bryant might have said it, then realized it was a woman's voice. Shaanáý's voice. His nerves tensed, and he stiffened in his seat.

He stared straight ahead, fearing that if he looked at Bryant his expression would give away his feelings. "What do I do?"

* * *

Hector called and cancelled the credit card he had used to secure the rental vehicles. It was in the name of John Smith. "You'll have fun trying to collect any fees for late return of the vehicles," he chuckled to himself.

Slinging on his backpack, Hector looked around one more time to make sure everything was in order. He trotted across the back yard and up the trail until it became steep. Then he walked as quickly as his breath would allow.

His phone rang. "Yes, everything is on schedule. Your package will be ready when you arrive." He said and hung up. "At least I hope it will be on time. Well, the timing is out of my control. I have to get everyone else ready."

Hector pushed on. "I will be glad to get back to warm Catalina."

* * *

Sam squirmed as Bryant drove toward the trailhead.

"It looks like you are getting antsy. We'll be OK. I'm sure I can handle Hector," Bryant said.

Sam started to reply with, "You underestimate Hector," when something in Bryant's voice caused his unease to crystallize into a realization. "Bryant is in league with Hector," he thought.

Fear gave way to rage when Sam decided he was in the car with an accomplice to Evie's abductor. He reached into his coat pocket and gripped the gun.

"That's why Hector left. He is waiting for Bryant to bring me to him. I'll know for sure if there are no officers waiting at the trailhead," ran through Sam's mind.

"I'm afraid you underestimate Hector," Sam finally responded.

"You may be underestimating me. I know a trick or two. Since there are two of us, we will approach him from two different angles so there is no way he can take both of us."

"I doubt we will see him," Sam said trying to play along. He thought about shooting Bryant as soon as they got out of the car. "I can't do that," he thought. "I don't even know why I think he is involved." He started to doubt himself. His heart insisted otherwise when they pulled up to the end of the street and there were no other officers waiting.

* * *

Hector was feeling happy as he approached the shelter. Rey cawed, announcing his presence. "Good afternoon to you, too," he said. He looked at his watch. "Four twenty-three. I made record time."

He stopped about twenty feet from the door of the shelter, pulled latex gloves out of his backpack, and put them on. "OK, people. It's time for your final performance."

"We're hungry. We need something to eat," David called out.

"You'll have plenty of time to worry about that later," Hector replied. "Here's the plan. I want you to come out one at a time, and we will move to your next location. It doesn't matter who goes first."

"What makes you think we would willingly do that?" Evie countered.

"Because it will be a lot less painful for you if you cooperate."

"What are you going to do with us? Are you going to kill us?" Sandi pleaded.

"No, I'm not going to kill you. Just move you to another spot. The view will be much better."

"He's lying," Viviana whispered.

"I'm sure you're right," James answered. "But I don't see what else we can do. I'll go first. If he kills me, stay in here and fight for your lives when he comes in."

"I'm coming out," James said without giving anyone time to protest. He walked out the door. Viviana kept it open to watch.

"Brave and wise," Hector said. "I appreciate you setting the example." He pulled handcuffs out of his backpack. "Hands behind your back, please."

Hector handcuffed James, then unlocked the cable from his shackles. "Right this way."

Hector held to the handcuffs and directed him east along the side of the shelter to a clearing of granite. There were six hemlock trees from which he had cut the bottom branches.

"Sit down with your back against this tree," Hector ordered. James complied. Hector looped a rope around James's chest and tied it behind the tree.

"Now I'm going to undo one wrist and cuff you behind the trunk. I expect you to cooperate." James didn't fight. Hector pulled James's arms around the tree and handcuffed him, then untied the rope. The trunk was small enough not to strain James's arms.

"I'll get you some company," Hector said and headed back to the shelter.

"Next," he called.

"I'll go," David said.

"I thought the saying was 'Ladies first,'" Hector said as David walked out. "But you'll do."

He handcuffed David and bent down to unlock the cable. He heard movement, and before he could respond, Viviana landed on his back and looped the cable around his neck, choking him.

As Hector started to stand, David knocked him over onto his right side. Viviana kept her hold on the cable. David grabbed Hector's right wrist and tried to hold it.

Hector's face was turning red. He didn't panic. He bent his left leg and planted the foot in the snow. With a powerful motion, Hector rolled onto his back, slinging David into Viviana and knocking her loose from the cable. He kept turning. In one motion he came up with his right hand and delivered a blow to David's face that sent him tumbling over Viviana and knocked him out.

Hector continued to turn and grabbed Viviana's hair with his right hand, pulling hard. "You are quite the problem child," he growled.

Viviana punched him in the gut, and Hector grabbed her by the throat with his left hand. "What are you going to do now?" he sneered just before she lost consciousness.

When she went limp, he tossed her into the snow. David was starting to move. Hector jerked him up by the handcuffs and dragged him to the clearing. David was still groggy when Hector plopped him down against next tree down from James. Hector didn't bother with the rope but quickly handcuffed David to the tree.

"Your friends are trying to get themselves killed," Hector said. "The Latina may have succeeded."

"You'd better hope she is OK," David managed to croak.

Hector glared at him and then laughed.

Chapter 39

As Sam reached for the door handle, he heard as clear as a bell, "Trust me. Go with him."

He looked toward Bryant but knew he hadn't said that. He wondered if he was going insane. "Or could this be the elders guiding me?" he considered.

"You look frightened," Bryant said across the car. "Are you sure you're up to this?"

"Where are the other officers?"

"I don't know. They should have been here. Let me check." Bryant pulled out his phone and dialed. "Bryant Stancil here. We're at the trail but have no back-up... I see." He disconnected.

"They were in a car crash on the way. Someone ran a red light. I don't think it's wise to wait for others to get here."

"I agree," Sam said with a certainty that surprised him. "Let's go."

Daséikw and Nadashée landed on Bryant's car and voiced their agreement.

Bryant opened the map on his phone. "One last check. Where do you think they are?"

Sam pointed to the location.

"So we will follow the trail then turn off to the left somewhere around here. I hope we can find them."

"I think Hector was staying in this house, "Sam said, pointing to the house where Hector had, in fact, been staying. "Maybe we should check it first." He led the way, and they looked through the windows. No one was there.

Sam spied the cornflower on the counter and thought, "That's odd."

He cupped his hands over his eyes and looked into the garage door. He felt a surge of adrenaline when he saw the white Hummer and gray Gladiator.

"His vehicles are here," he called out. "Let's go up the trail."

He headed back to the trail access with Bryant right behind. He paused and decided he wanted to stay behind Bryant. "After you," he said, gesturing toward the trail. Bryant set off.

Sam felt more than saw the change in light as the sun dropped and dusk began to deepen. They reached the point where the snow began and footprints emerged.

"I don't think it will take a rocket scientist to find them," Bryant said.

Desperation began to gather in Sam's soul, his darkening mood mimicking the fading light. He wanted to run to get there as quickly as possible but knew he would give out. He was grateful that Bryant set a quick but sustainable pace.

He tried to picture in his mind what he would find when he got there. "She has to be alive. I can't picture any alternative," he thought.

Thinking of Evie drove Sam faster till he almost ran into Bryant. Bryant looked back. "Are you OK?" he asked.

"I was thinking and not paying attention. I guess I'm in a hurry," Sam said. He dropped back a few paces and resumed thinking.

"If Bryant is with Hector, it will be two against one when I get there. What am I going to do? I can't shoot Bryant. He may be innocent. I will shoot Hector if I get the chance. I can't see any way around that. But I will have to aim for something other than his chest."

They kept walking and the snow began to deepen. The uphill climb caused Sam to breathe hard and drew him out of his thoughts. Up ahead, he saw the point where the footprints veered off the trail.

Bryant stopped. "We're getting closer. As soon as we see signs of Hector or the captives, we are going to split up. I want you to watch me. I'm not going to say a word, and I need for you to keep quiet, too. I will point to where I want you to go. Coming from two different angles will give us the best chance to capture this guy."

Sam nodded that he understood. But at the same time, uncertainty filled his soul. "Bryant sure is convincing that he is on my side. I have no reason to doubt him other than these strange voices in my head and my gut."

As if on cue, he heard Shaanáy's voice, "It's time." Like the sun breaking through clouds, Sam knew what he had to do.

He grasped the gun in his pocket and crept close to Bryant. Without a word he pulled out the gun and whacked Bryant on the head, knocking him out.

Worried, Sam knelt to make sure he was still breathing. He was. Sam set off with urgency to finally bring this nightmare to an end.

He followed the footprints in the snow for a while, trying to decide how to attack Hector. "I should probably shoot first and ask questions later," he thought. Then he stopped.

"What would Viviana do? Walking in on the trail would be exactly what Hector expects, particularly if Bryant has let him know we are coming. But Bryant was going to send me off the trail. I think Viviana would take a different approach. In western movies, they always want the high ground. Maybe there is wisdom in that."

He eyed the terrain, then pushed uphill. It was tough going in the deep snow. He slipped and slid down about ten feet. Other than a cut on his hand, he seemed to be OK.

He kept fighting until he was as high as he could get and still make out the footprints in the snow below. Then he proceeded in the direction the trail led. Daséikw and Nadashée floated silently above.

"Maybe I have a chance with their help," Sam thought. "I need your help, too, Lord," he breathed a quick prayer.

He walked as quietly as he could, moving his eyes from what was up ahead to the trail below to make sure he didn't get off track.

The farther he walked, the more tense he became. "Failure is not an option. I have to save Evie and the others."

Walking in the deep snow was strenuous and slow. He felt he would never get there.

* * *

Hector carried Viviana to the clearing and slammed her against the tree. "I don't care whether this one wakes up or not," he said.

"What are you going to do with us?" David asked.

"You will find out soon enough."

Sandi was the last one Hector brought out. She was wide-eyed with fear and seemed to have no hope left.

"This is what the bosses wanted," Hector explained as he handcuffed her to a tree.

He stood back and admired his work. "That is quite a sight," he said. "Now, one more to go."

Chapter 40

Sam continued to push forward. He could still make out the trail below but saw nothing but woods ahead. He was starting to doubt himself and wonder if he had come the wrong way when Daséikw landed silently in the snow in front of him.

Sam knelt down and followed the raven's gaze. At first, he saw nothing but woods. He looked back at Daséikw and saw that he was still focused on the same area.

He looked hard and finally noticed something that looked like a hut through the trees. He whispered, "Thanks," to Daséikw.

Dusk continued to deepen, making it harder to see. Without moving, Sam watched, searching for Hector.

He saw movement. Something came from beyond the shelter. In Sam's mind it was a brown coat. He tensed. "Hector," he hissed.

He waited and watched but didn't see Hector come out from behind the shelter. "Is he hiding? Does he know I'm here?" Sam wondered.

He decided it was time to move and began creeping closer to the shelter. When he was directly above it, he began to move downhill. He stopped when he saw movement. "That's definitely Hector," he thought. He watched as Hector walked away from the shelter back the way he had come.

When he was out of sight, Sam moved to the front of the shelter. Hearing nothing, he opened the door. His heart sank when he saw no one. "They're not here," he cringed. In the dim light, he thought he could make out sleeping bags scattered along the floor.

"He has moved them," he thought, his heart sinking. He went to the corner and peered around in the direction he had last seen Hector move.

* * *

After cuffing Sandi to the tree, Hector hustled back to the shelter and fished a duffle bag from the snow beside it. He returned and started with Sandi.

"Sit down with your legs straight," he ordered. He removed the shackles and put them into the wet duffle bag. "Next," he said, moving to Evie.

"You'll never get away with this," Evie said.

"And exactly what are you going to do about it?" Hector asked and laughed.

Hector stood and listened. "Ah, my ride is coming. We're waiting on one more package. Then I can get out of here." The sound of a helicopter grew gradually louder.

* * *

Looking from the corner of the shelter, Sam could see footprints leading away. He listened. Something strange registered in his ears. "What is that?"

The sound grew, and Sam recognized it as a helicopter. "I wonder if that's good news or bad."

He pondered his next move and decided just to follow the prints in the snow. He checked to make sure the safety was off, gripped the pistol tightly, and moved out.

He came around a bend and could see Hector kneeling by a tree. "What is he doing?" Then he saw Evie. She was sitting by a tree and Hector was taking something off her legs. Sam couldn't make out what it was in the twilight.

The sound of the helicopter intensified. Sam decided this was his chance. He hurried toward Hector and, before Hector could stand, Sam hollered, "Don't move!"

Hector looked up at Sam and smiled. "You're right on time."

Sam wanted to shoot, but Sandi was in his line of fire behind Hector. He couldn't risk hitting her.

Hector started to stand. "I said don't move!" Sam yelled over the growing thump of the helicopter.

"You have already shot me once, and yet here we are," Hector said.

"I'm not aiming at your vest," Sam said with his pistol directed at Hector's head.

"You wouldn't want to be the cause of this pretty lady's death, would you?"

"No, but I would be happy to be the cause of yours. Now back away from Evie and lie on the ground."

"I'm afraid I can't do that." Before Sam knew what was happening, Hector lunged behind the tree and had Evie's head in his hands.

"Now this is getting interesting. Will you shoot and risk missing? If you miss, I will snap her neck in two. Or you can put down the gun and lie face down on the ground like a good boy."

Sam was standing at the edge of the clearing. He could see all the others. Time froze as his mind raced through options. "Shoot. Do what he says and hope for another option. Act like I'm going to lie down to get closer, then shoot."

A terrifying idea registered, and Sam knew it was right. He walked into the clearing directly in front of Evie.

"So what's it to be?" Hector asked.

Sam put the gun to his own temple. "Step away from Evie, or I shoot."

"That's interesting," Hector replied.

"You need me alive to get your paycheck. Step away from Evie."

Hector let go of Evie and stood behind the hemlock.

"Sam, no!" Evie protested.

"Now what?" Hector asked.

"Come out and lie face down right here," Sam said pointing with his left hand.

"And if I don't?"

"I'm going to die either way. At least this way I can ruin your chance of getting paid."

Sam could barely hear the others shouting over the helicopter. He dared not take his eyes off Hector.

Hector moved around the tree. "OK. You win."

Sam kept the pistol to his temple, watching Hector. Suddenly someone grabbed his right arm and jerked it away from his head.

"Drop it," a voice yelled into Sam's ear as a pistol pushed against his head. He knew the voice. It was Bryant. He felt his life draining from his body. He looked at Evie, and she held his gaze with a love that spoke forgiveness. But the feeling of failure was overwhelming.

Before he knew what was happening, Hector was on him. Sam felt the gun wrenched from his hand. He was falling toward the ground. He had no resistance left.

He looked over and saw Evie's tears. "I'm sorry," he said.

He felt the handcuffs go on and felt himself dragged to his feet. Somehow he no longer seemed to be part of his body. As if from the air, he saw himself dragged to the tree and handcuffed to it.

He could see Hector shaking hands with Bryant. Bryant rubbed his head. Daséikw landed on Sam's shoulder. Sam could hear him cawing, but it was Shaanáy̓'s voice.

"From death comes new life. From weakness, strength. From defeat, victory. Embrace your journey."

Sam realized Hector was standing over him. Daséikw launched and gouged Hector in the eye. He swatted at the raven and cursed.

Sam struggled to his feet. Hector punched him in the gut, and Sam bent and coughed from the pain.

"That's for the bird," Hector said.

Sam forced himself upright. "So you think you have won. I trust the truth of what you are doing here will haunt you the rest of your life."

Hector smiled. "It will haunt me all the way to the bank."

"I don't think any amount of money will ease your soul for murdering six innocent people."

"You have it all wrong. I'm not murdering anyone. I'm leaving. It will be left up to starvation, exposure, bears, or wolves to do the killing. All I did was wrap up a package for my employer, you see."

"You will be a miserable soul for the rest of your life, which may not be very long."

"Pardon me a moment while I shake with fear," Hector said and laughed.

Chapter 41

The sound of the helicopter stopped. Hector was packing the last of the shackles into the duffle bag when Sam heard two engines crank up. The sounds got closer, and soon he could see two snowmobiles coming along a trail under the peak of the mountain.

As they pulled into the clearing, Sam recognized the drivers: Mitch Carter and Holmes Harrison. They cut the engines and stepped off.

"Just as you ordered," Hector said, shaking hands with the two men.

Mitch Carter walked up to Sam and grinned. "Now you will learn the price of crossing your superiors. You will get to watch as these other five slowly die. Then you will join them."

"Yes, this is what it costs to tamper with our plans," Harrison added. "Each of you chose to risk your lives to foil the effort to expand my business. Now you will regret your actions for as long as it takes you to die."

"Revenge is so sweet," Carter said. "I must admit, I wasn't sure you could pull this off, Hector. But you did, and we are grateful."

"And my money?" Hector asked.

"It's on the helicopter just as you asked. Plus, there is a five per cent bonus for your perfect execution," Harrison said.

"It's getting dark and I would hate to get stuck up here like you," Carter said looking at Sam.

"Let the others go. I was the one who caused all your problems," Sam said.

Carter laughed. "I know you were the ring leader. That's why the others have been starved and weakened. You will get to watch them die first."

Sam's heart sank and seemed to stop beating. He lunged at Carter, but the tree held him fast. Carter laughed. The world went blurry. A misty form of Shaanáý appeared. She seemed to be across the clearing.

She was speaking. "Tell this obnoxious soul you have foreseen that he won't get off the mountain."

The world slowly came back into focus. Sam could hear Evie calling, "Sam, are you OK?"

"I'm OK," he answered. "I have just received a message for these four: You won't make it off the mountain tonight."

Carter and Harrison looked at each other and laughed. Sam saw an amused grin on Hector's face.

"I suppose you are going to stop us," Harrison chuckled.

"You won't be laughing long," Sam retorted.

"We need to go," Hector said. He walked up to Sam and jingled the keys to the handcuffs. "I don't think we'll be needing these." He threw them down the mountain.

Hector hopped onto one of the snowmobiles. "I'm looking forward to some tropical warmth on a nice beach."

"I need to go, too," Bryant said. "My cover has been blown."

Harrison looked at Carter. "OK. We'll find something to do with you," Carter said.

Sam started hearing crows in the trees around him. Rey, Daséikw, Nadashée, Canto, and Kat landed in the clearing. Another raven landed at Evie's feet and looked her in the eye.

"Hey, there," Evie said.

Rey and Daséikw were cawing back and forth to each other. The new raven went over to them. Sam thought it seemed a serious conversation.

Hector and Harrison cranked the snowmobiles, and Bryant and Carter got on behind them. When they took off, all the birds except Canto launched and flew toward the mountain peak.

Sam watched as at least fifty more crows and ravens fell in with them. They flew to the deep snow near the peak. Sam could see black dots. They seemed to be scratching frantically.

"Look!" Sam said to the others.

Viviana had just regained consciousness and asked, "What are you talking about?"

"The birds on the mountain," Evie said, gesturing with her chin.

As they watched, snow began to roll down the mountain. It gathered more and more snow as it went. Soon it was an avalanche. Before long, Sam heard the roar of the crashing snow.

"Does anyone have any doubt that the avalanche landed on Harrison and Carter?" Sam asked.

"Nope," David said. "I believe that is the end of them."

"Good riddance," Evie said.

"That is something to celebrate. But I hate to point out the fact that we can't give each other high fives," James said.

"The birds may have taken them out, but they have also succeeded in taking us out," David observed.

"What are we going to do?" Sandi said. "I don't think I can stand this."

"First of all, let's not panic," Sam said searching for hope. "Joe was going to meet us at the trail. I'm sure he will find us. The footprints are so obvious even I was able to follow them."

"Is that true, or are you just saying that?" Sandi challenged.

"It is true," Sam said.

They waited silently. Sam hoped he was right and that Joe would follow. "He will see Bryant's car there," he thought. "Unless Bryant texted him not to come." The last thought was like a rope squeezing Sam's heart. Light took another step back as night approached.

"What if Joe doesn't come because it's getting dark?" Sandi asked.

Sam could sense her panic rising. "That's not the Joe I know. He'll come."

"At least we have a pretty view. Until it gets dark, that is," David said.

Sam looked out at the mountains. "David's right. Let's try to appreciate the scenery. How many mountains can you count?"

"Don't ask me to count the trees next," Viviana said.

Time crawled second by second. Night took another step forward. The birds returned to the clearing.

Rey hopped over to Viviana. "We need help, mi amigo."

Rey gave her a look that Sam interpreted as, "I'm already on it."

"Where did Canto go?" David asked. "I hope he didn't get caught in the avalanche."

"I'm sure he's OK," Evie said.

As if on cue, Sam heard jingling coming from across the clearing. Canto hopped up the hill into view carrying the keys Hector had thrown.

"Way to go Canto!" David said.

Canto hopped over, struggling with the weight of the keys. He laid them at David's feet.

"Thank you, my friend. You are a hero!"

"I hate to point this out, but you still can't reach them," Sandi said.

David pushed into standing and worked the keys to the back of the tree with his foot. Gauging their location, he sat down and began trying to unlock his cuffs. He dropped the keys twice before finally getting one in the lock.

"Ladies and gentlemen, thanks to some brilliant birds, we are free!" David said as he stepped away from the tree. He went straight to Viviana and kissed her.

"That's nice, but get me loose," she said.

David moved from tree to tree unlocking the cuffs. Sam and Evie embraced. "I was so afraid I had lost you," Sam said.

"I knew you would find me. I could sense it," Evie said.

"I know it feels good to be free," James said. "But it is getting dark. We need to go."

As they walked past the shelter Viviana said, "I'm getting my arrows. "

"I'm never setting foot inside there again," Sandi said.

Sam led the way as they tromped through the snow, retracing step by step the path of terror that had brought each one to their grueling imprisonment. Everyone walked in silence. Sam hoped the fear, panic, and suffering would be left behind with each step, but he knew that wasn't likely.

A little way after they rejoined the Indian River Trail, Sam stopped. "Shaanáý?"

"I see you have learned well. You will be a great chief."

"What is it, Sam?" Evie asked.

"This is Shaanáý," he said pointing to where he had seen her.

"I don't see anyone," Evie said. "Are you sure you're OK?"

Sam looked back and Shaanáý was gone. He smiled. "Yes, I am very OK."

About half a mile down the trail they met Joe.

"What in the world!" Joe said. "How did you escape?"

Rey cawed from a tree above them.

"Yes, Rey, I'll tell him about you," Sam said. "We had the help of some brilliant birds."

"Where is the assassin?"

"I'm afraid you have some bodies to retrieve on the mountain. The birds caused an avalanche that buried Hector, Carter, Harrison, and Bryant."

"What? Why was Bryant with them? Wait, do you mean Holmes Harrison and Mitch Carter were here, too?"

"It's a long story. I'll fill you in on the way down," Sam said.

Joe turned and led them down the trail.

"By the way, did you pass an old woman with long gray hair?" Sam asked.

"No," Joe said giving him a look as if he had lost it. "I think we need to get all of you checked out at the hospital."

Chapter 42

Joe radioed ahead to have ambulances waiting at the trailhead and to let the captives' families know they were OK and were coming home.

Sam could see the flashing lights of the ambulances long before they got to the road. "I don't think I need an ambulance," he said.

"Me, either. I just want to see Tamara," James said.

The others echoed the thought.

"I think you need to get checked out," David said to Viviana. "Those are nasty bruises on your cheeks. Something might be broken."

"Viviana is a warrior. She did battle with that brute," Sandi said.

When they got to the light of the ambulances, Joe said, "I agree with David. You look rough. Please at least get x-rayed."

"OK," Viviana agreed.

"I'm riding with you," David said.

"Sam, I think you need to get checked out, too," Joe said.

"I'm OK."

"You don't seem quite right in the head," Joe argued.

"Are you talking about the old woman?"

"Yeah," Joe said.

"Trust me, I'm more right in the head than I have ever been," Sam replied.

"What do you think, Evie?" Joe asked.

"He did seem to have a hallucination on the trail. Are you sure you're OK?"

"I'm fine."

"I trust Sam's judgment," Evie said. "I'll keep an eye on him for anything suspicious."

"OK," Joe said. "I'm going to check on you tomorrow, though, if that's OK."

"Sure," Sam answered.

Tamara arrived and nearly knocked James over when she ran into his arms. "I'm so sorry. I was afraid I would never see you again," she said through her tears.

"That was my fear, too," James said. "I wasn't ready to move on to the next life without you."

Sandi and Stan embraced, too. "Are you OK?" Stan asked.

"Hungry, scared, and tired. But other than that I think I'm fine."

"Is one of these ambulances for Sandi?" Stan called out.

"Yes," Joe said.

"I don't need an ambulance. Just take me home."

"I think she'll be OK," David said. "She's quite a trouper."

As David and Viviana crawled into the ambulance, Sam called out, "We'll be by to pick you up from the emergency room."

"Thanks," David said. "It would be a long walk home."

Sandra rushed up and grabbed Sam. Skauty followed with a long hug for Evie.

"Do either of you need to go to the ER?" Skauty asked.

"I'm not hurt. Just hungry and tired," Evie said.

"What about you, Sam?"

"I don't seem to have any injuries, either. But I could use something to eat. It's been a long day."

"Let's get you home then," Sandra said.

As they pulled up to the house, Nadashée, Daséikw and the other raven landed on the roof.

"Another new bird friend?" Skauty asked.

"It looks like it," Sam said. "I think we've been adopted."

"A raven is the perfect bird for a Tlingit clan leader," Skauty pointed out.

"Shaanáý said that Daséikw is an ancient bird," Sam said.

"You met Shaanáý?" Skauty asked.

"Yes. She was out on the side of a mountain."

"That's interesting," Skauty said.

They walked into the house, and Sam plunked down into a kitchen chair. "Man, I'm tired. This has been quite an ordeal."

Evie sat down next to him. Sandra got busy warming a pot of soup she had made before they had to leave the house.

"The strangest thing about this ordeal was thinking we were going to die," Evie said. "It wasn't as frightening as I would have thought it would be."

"I don't know about that," Sam said. "When I saw you handcuffed to the tree, I was terrified. And then there was nothing I could do. I felt so helpless, so defeated."

"But you were thinking about my death, not yours. I had plenty of time to ponder my own death. I found myself thinking about the good things that have happened. There were some regrets and heartaches, but overall my life has been good. That brought peace. I don't think I could have stayed sane chained in the shelter without that peace."

Sam looked at Evie and love surged in his heart. "I'm glad you had that peace," he said. "And I'm glad I have you back."

Sandra served up steaming bowls of soup. "You will have to tell us all about it. But right now I think soup and some rest are in order."

Sam and Evie scarfed down their soup as quickly as they could get it cool enough.

"I have to go pick up David and Viviana at the ER," Sam said. By the time he had finished his soup, his face was nearly planted in the bowl. Evie slid his bowl out of the way.

"I don't think you are going anywhere but to bed," Skauty said. "I'll get them home."

Sam didn't respond. He was asleep.

"Sam Hanson, you wake up and come upstairs with me," Evie chided. She shook him awake and led him upstairs. "I think you need a good night's sleep. How long have you been awake?"

"I'm not sure," Sam mumbled.

Evie helped him change clothes and get into the bed.

"Aren't you coming to bed?" he asked.

"Not till I've had a shower. I feel nasty."

Sam was asleep before she got out of the room. Evie hustled through the shower, then snuggled up next to Sam.

Sam awoke and looked at his watch. It said 8:03. "I guess I napped for a couple of hours. It feels longer than that. Wait, it's morning!" He was amazed when he realized daylight was coming through the window.

Evie stirred next to him. "I hope you slept as well as I did."

"I feel like we just lay down."

"Ummm." She pulled Sam close and held him. "This is so much nicer than that shack."

"I can't imagine how horrible that must have been."

"I don't want to think about that right now. I just want to snuggle with my hero."

"Actually, the birds are the heroes."

"You don't even realize what you did, do you?"

"I tried to save you, but I failed."

"Sam, you gathered the force of nature and brought it to that mountain. The birds and the avalanche were there because of you. And because of you, Joe was there with a light as it was getting dark."

"No, I don't think that was me."

"I'm sure you had some help from above, but without you we would all be dying on that mountain this morning."

"Hmmm. I sure don't want to think about that!" He snuggled closer.

Chapter 43

It's about time you two stirred," Sandra said as Sam and Evie came into the kitchen. "I took the liberty of inviting everyone for lunch to celebrate having you back safe and sound."

"Everyone?" Sam asked.

"Well, you know. The usual crew."

"Thanks, Sandra," Evie said. "It will be nice to celebrate our unshackled selves."

"Is Grandpa coming? I need to talk to him," Sam said.

"Nope, he's already here," Skauty said as he walked into the kitchen. "You don't think I'd miss a free breakfast!"

Sandra set plates of pancakes and poured coffee for everyone.

"You don't have to wait on us, Mom," Sam said.

"Well, don't get used to it, but I think you deserve it today," she replied.

"Grandpa, some weird things happened to me while I was trying to save Evie and the others."

"Yes, you said you met Shaanáý."

"I don't see how a woman that old could get that far out in the woods. And then I saw her on the mountain where we were all chained to trees. I'm amazed she could walk that far. It was a hard hike for me."

"I see," Skauty said. "Do you know the meaning of her name?"

"I think she said it means valley."

"Yes. Like, 'Yea, though I walk through the valley of the shadow of death, I will fear no evil: for thou art with me.' Legend says that Shaanáÿ is spirit."

"You mean she wasn't really there? But I was so sure she was real."

"She was real, all right. More real than anything we can touch."

"See, I told you that you had help from above," Evie said.

Sam had goosebumps on his arms. "Once when Daséikw cawed, I could hear Shaanáÿ speaking."

There was a knock on the door, and David and Viviana popped in. "We couldn't wait till lunch to check on our hero," David said.

"Viviana, are you OK?" Evie said jumping up to hug her. Viviana was sporting a serious black eye."

"I'll live," she said. "They said there is a small fracture in my cheek bone, but it will heal without any treatment."

"I kind of like her new look," David said.

Viviana punched him in the chest.

"Ouch! I guess I deserved that."

"Yes, you did," Evie said.

"Pancakes?" Sandra asked.

"No thanks. We've already had breakfast, but coffee sure would be nice," David said and aimed for the coffee pot.

"Sam was just telling us about meeting Shaanáÿ," Evie said. Grandpa says she is kind of like the Holy Spirit."

"I remember reading about her somewhere," David said. "You mean you actually saw her?"

"I did. Well, at least I thought I saw her."

"He saw her twice," Evie said.

"Actually, it was four times."

"Do tell all," David said.

"While I was trying to get away from Hector, I hid in a cave in the Russian Orthodox Cemetery."

"Wait, what do you mean you were trying to get away from Hector?" David asked.

"OK, let me back up. Joe had moved us to a different house to try to hide us from Hector. He's the assassin that abducted everyone."

"Yeah, I figured that out."

"After he found us and took Evie, I got a message from Solar Wind that I needed to come to him. I found him way out on a mountain. He had this crazy idea that if I stayed safe and let all of you die, he could convince the government to overturn the monopolies of the A-30. He didn't think Hector could find me there, but somehow he did. I got away, and the chase was on. That's how I ended up in the cemetery."

"I see," David said.

"Hector was closing in when I found this cave and crawled in. There was a bear hibernating, and I hid behind it. Hector came in and the bear scared him off. After that, I'm not sure what happened, but I thought I saw the spirits of former chiefs appearing.

"They came and placed their hands on my shoulders. It was such a solemn moment. Dad was there. You were there, too, Grandpa. You assured me I could free the others. Then Shaanáý was there and said, 'See what happens when you listen?'"

"Wow!" David said. "We are surrounded by such a great cloud of witnesses."

"I have heard it said that the spirits of elders have appeared to chiefs in the past. It is considered a sign that the chief will be great."

Sam had goosebumps again.

Another knock on the door, and James and Tamara came in. "You're still eating breakfast? It's almost eleven o'clock," James teased. "Actually, we slept late, too."

"Thanks for inviting us for lunch," Tamara said.

"I wouldn't have it any other way," Sandra replied. "After what you all have been through, we need to be together."

"You were put through the worry wringer," David said. "I'm sure that was hard, too."

"There wasn't anything fun about it," Sandra said. "But it's over now. Let's just enjoy each other's company."

"After lunch, I need to hike up and check on Jolly," Sam said. "I heard shots fired after I left his cabin. Since Hector was very much alive, I fear he might have been shot."

"I'll go with you," David said. "After being cooped up in that shack, I need to stretch my legs."

"I'll come, too," James said. "We may have to carry a body down."

The women looked at each other. "Nah, I'm staying here," Evie said. "I've had enough of the great outdoors for a while."

Sam, David, and James drove to the trailhead where Hector had parked and hiked up the trail toward Jolly's.

The snow had crusted over during the night and made a loud crunch as they walked.

"It's a good thing we don't have to sneak up on anyone," James said.

Sam found the tracks where he had turned off the trail and had met Jolly. "It seems like so long ago that I was here. But it was just yesterday. That was the longest day of my life."

"I hope it remains the longest," David quipped.

About a tenth of a mile from the shack, Sam grinned. Up ahead he could see a dark figure in a black hood with long stringy hair sticking out.

He started to run but after a few paces noticed a shotgun at the ready. He stopped.

"Hey, Jolly! It's Sam. I came to see if you are OK." He kept walking forward.

"Why wouldn't I be OK?" Jolly called.

"I heard shots after I left. When I saw Hector, I was afraid he had shot you."

For the first time, Sam saw Jolly smile.

"Yeah, that was me shooting. He came back like I said he would. I told him you were gone, but he didn't believe me. He kept coming till my rifle convinced him otherwise."

"You can put the gun down," Sam said.

"Why did you bring all these people with you?"

"We thought we might have to carry you down the mountain," David said.

"How neighborly," Jolly grumped. "Thor, here."

The husky appeared from behind Sam, David, and James and joined Jolly.

"Thanks for calling him in."

"Is that your place?" David asked. "That is cool!"

"Do you mind if we come in for a minute?" Sam asked.

"I only have two chairs."

"That's OK. We won't be long."

Jolly turned and went into the cabin. Sam and the others followed.

"What is it?" Jolly asked. Thor stood beside him carefully watching.

"Hector is dead. So are Harrison and Carter," Sam said.

"I know. Stancil, too."

"I'm sorry I ruined your plan," Sam said.

"We'll see."

"Is there anything we can do for you?" David asked.

"No."

"Jolly, if you decide you want to come and live in town, we will welcome you. If not, let me know if you ever need anything."

"I won't. OK."

"Do you have Sam's number?" James asked.

"Don't need it."

"Thanks so much for your help. I don't think we would have survived without you," Sam said.

"You're welcome."

Sam turned to go. When he put his hand on the door, he looked back. "What is your real name?"

"Jolly will do."

Chapter 44

It was 4:11 when Sam, James, and David got back to the house. They found everyone in the den watching the news.

"What's up?" Sam asked.

"They're talking about the avalanche," Evie said.

"An anonymous source reported that Holmes Harrison and Mitch Carter, both members of the A-30, were buried in a tragic avalanche on The Sisters Mountain in Alaska yesterday.

"Police and National Guard forces have launched a rescue mission but have not located them yet. They are presumed most likely dead. Two other men were reported to be with them, one of them possibly an internationally-known assassin named Hector Hoffman. We will bring you further coverage of this story as details emerge."

"I wonder if they will ever find the bodies. That was a lot of snow!" James said.

"I'm sure they will," Evie said.

"How could you know that?" James asked.

"Trust me. When Evie says they will, they will." They all laughed.

The next morning after breakfast, Sam and Evie went to the store to get Sam a new phone. Sam studied over the phones and gravitated to the most expensive one.

"Can a man without a job afford that?" Evie pointed out.

"I guess you're right."

"I'm teasing. If that's what you want, get it. I'm sure employment opportunities will soon present themselves."

"I was thinking about buying a plane and carrying on Dad's business."

Evie gave him an "I can't believe you just said that" look. "Really? You have to be kidding. I think you need to stick to what you know."

"I know how to fly a plane."

"But you don't know anything about running a business.

"Well, that's true," Sam admitted.

The dealer activated the phone, and Sam and Evie left. As the Tesla pulled into the garage, Sam's phone pinged.

"Check the news. >>>>Solar Wind"

"That didn't take long! I got a message from Jolly saying to check the news."

They hustled inside and turned it on. "Joe Ford, Chief of Sitka Police, made a statement alleging that Holmes Harrison and Mitch Carter were involved in a scheme to assassinate six people who may have thwarted some of their business deals.

"Spokespeople for both Global Food Source and MC2 deny the allegations. They say the two men were on a hunting expedition. We will keep you updated as we learn more."

"Oh no!"

"What, Sam?" Evie asked.

"I hope they don't come after Joe now."

"You're right. We'd better warn him."

Sam called. "Hey, Joe. Have you seen the news?... I wanted to warn you that the MC2 and GFS organizations may come after you."

"Thanks, but I thought about that before I made my statement. The world needs to know the truth. I'll be careful."

Sam disconnected. "He already knew that was a possibility but made the statement anyway."

"He's a good man," Evie said.

The next morning, Sam turned on the news right after breakfast. "Four bodies and two snowmobiles have just been unearthed near Sitka, Alaska. The four men are identified as Mitch

Carter, head of MC2, Holmes Harrison, head of Global Food Source, Hector Hoffman, and Bryant Stancil, a member of the Alaska Bureau of Investigation.

"The National Guard are transporting the bodies to a morgue in Sitka for autopsies before they are released to the families."

"I'm glad they found the bodies," Evie said. "It's better for the families. Besides, it would be too creepy knowing they are still up there."

"You're right. I wonder if someone like Hector even has a family."

A knock on the door interrupted their conversation. Sam answered it to find three men in dark suits standing at the door.

"Sam Hanson?" the man in front asked.

"Yes, that's me."

"You are being subpoenaed to appear before a Congressional investigative committee on February twenty-eighth at ten am. You will find all the details in these documents. I need your signature to certify that the subpoena has been delivered."

"What is this about?" Sam asked.

"I'm not at liberty to reveal details," the man said.

"That's OK. I'm sure I know." Sam signed, took the documents, and closed the door.

"What was that about?" Evie asked.

"Jolly did it!"

"Did what?"

"He got Congress to investigate the A-30!"

"Wow! We'll be living in a new country soon! I told you that you will be a great chief!"

There was another knock at the door. "I wonder who that is?" Sam said. He opened the door, and there stood George Janson.

"Hey, Sam."

"Hey, George." Sam looked beyond and saw cars lining up, parking along the side of the road. "What's up?"

"I wanted to come and apologize. I was terribly wrong. Anyone who could save the lives of all those people is a worthy leader. I want you to know that you have my full support."

"Thank you so much, George. You don't know how much that means to me."

"What is this?" Skauty said over Sam's shoulder as Sam stepped out the door.

"It looks like I'm not the only one coming to thank Sam for what he did," George responded.

People gathered in the front yard, and a line began to form.

"I don't think you have to worry about having the clan's support any longer," Skauty said.

A NOTE FROM THE AUTHOR

Thank you so much for letting me share this story with you. I have enjoyed writing the Dark Wings books. The characters have become a part of me over the years. I hope you enjoyed Sam's story of reclaiming his Tlingit identity.

Please take a moment to leave a review of the book on the site from which you purchased it and/or Goodreads. Reviews help other folks gauge whether or not the book is right for them.

Rey says he will stay on the job and try to keep these humans safe as long as he is able.

9 781736 139547